CONFIRMED KILL

KILL

DIRECT HIT

MIKE MORRIS

D1558743

DIAMOND BOOKS, NEW YORK

This book is a Diamond original edition, and has never been previously published.

DIRECT HIT

A Diamond Book / published by arrangement with the author

PRINTING HISTORY
Diamond edition / February 1993

ISBN: 1-55773-815-7

Diamond Books are published by The Berkley Publishing Group,
200 Madison Avenue, New York, NY 10016.
The name "DIAMOND" and its logo are trademarks
belonging to Charter Communications, Inc.

PRINTED IN THE UNITED STATES OF AMERICA

10 9 8 7 6 5 4 3 2 1

ASSAULT ON PARADISE

Explosions rocked the ridge above them as the *Whisper* began to work over all possible targets. Penelope watched in fascination as tracers lit up the sky. A bullet hit the tower and she started across the beach, moving in crisscross little runs of 15 to 20 feet.

As she drew even with the dock, a gun roared and flashed from aboard the cigarette boat. She felt an impact in her shoulder and was knocked violently to the ground.

Hit. She'd been hit. A rush of pain swept over her, the rusty smell of fresh blood, her blood, assailing her nostrils . . .

CONFIRMED KILL
Direct Hit

SPECIAL PREVIEW!
Turn to the back of this book for a special excerpt from an exciting new military series . . .

AIRBORNE

. . . an epic saga in the bestselling tradition of W. E. B. Griffin's *Brotherhood of War*.

Diamond Books by Mike Morris

CONFIRMED KILL
SNIPER SHOT
DIRECT HIT

1

"Please follow me, Mr. Brooks. Your table is ready, near the large windows, just as you requested."

"Very good, young man," said Martin Brooks, a.k.a. Peter Coy Booker, as he pressed a fifty-dollar bill into the man's pocket.

"Thank *you*, sir."

"Not at all. The view is certainly worth it."

Only the week before, Peter Coy Booker had resumed his life after leaving the expensive, reconstructive surgical wing of Highgate Hempstead Hospital outside London. He had a completely new face and a sinister-looking leather "hand" that filled what would otherwise be an empty glove. He had lost the hand in his ill-fated attempt at political assassination in Folkestone Harbor.

Fifteen months ago, Peter Booker had been blasted into the water by the fresh new weapons and tactics of an old foe, Con Duggan, field leader of the secret Confirmed Kill Team. Con Duggan now thought Peter Coy Booker was dead. In a sense, he was, since, as Martin Brooks, he and his associates were sitting in a public ballroom on New Year's Eve less than twenty feet away from Con Duggan and his celebratory party.

Con Duggan looked briefly across the small distance

1

between the tables. He smiled, as if at someone he recognized.

"Martin Brooks" smiled back. He was no longer Peter Coy Booker. But he was here, at the right time and place, to destroy Con Duggan's Confirmed Kill Team, and finally, when the last measure of psychological revenge had been taken, he'd kill Con Duggan himself. It began here, tonight, with Maggie Stuart, Con Duggan's companion of over twenty years. He would begin the destruction of the team by breaking the spirit of its leader. He knew Con Duggan valued Maggie above all other things in life, so taking her away from him would be sweet indeed.

He ordered a magnum of champagne for the Confirmed Kill Team table, and enclosed his card which read, MARTIN BROOKS, ENGINEERING/ARMAMENTS CONSULTANT. To Con Duggan's quizzical stare, he tipped his glass and smiled. Soon he'd know how good his plastic surgeon really was. If Con saw nothing but Martin Brooks when they met, Maggie Stewart was as good as sacked and delivered.

"Do you know him, Con?"

Con studied the card, trying to attach their benefactor's name and business with his face. "He looks vaguely familiar, yes, but I can't place him, and with that leather-hand gizmo, I'm sure I'd remember."

Sitting at Con Duggan's table were the principal members of the Confirmed Kill Team. Steven Dye and Penelope were there, as was Michael Barns, on one of the few occasions the boss mixed socially with the hired help. Con had brought Maggie, of course, and Maggie's father, United States Senator Parker Champion Stuart, who preferred to be called "Champ," had shown up on his own. It would seem to be the ideal, if irritating, mix for a very lively time.

On the street twenty stories below, Chin K. Lee, Booker's number-one henchman and martial arts *sensai*, parked a van painted like an ambulance at the service exit of the hotel. Dressed as paramedics, Chin and two other men sat quietly in the van, waiting for a signal from Booker, who was equipped with a miniature transceiver hidden in his leather hand. They had been able to do only one practice run, but the plan for snatching Maggie Stuart from the ballroom was a simple one. Still, it would have to work the first time.

New Year's Eve revelers passed by the van in a colorful stream of evening dresses and tuxedoes, paying little attention to it. Somehow, it seemed perfectly natural parked there, its overhead emergency lights off, its parking lights blinking. New Year's Eve and ambulances with medical technicians were a natural mix. There was a soft, light mist, and the van's wipers made a gentle swishing sound as they moved at low speed, one step ahead of the rain. Maggie's pumpkin was primed and ready.

The Ballroom
11:35 P.M.

"A pretty dazzling crowd, Senator. Not my actual cup o' tea, but . . . interesting." Penelope James, sitting directly across the table from Maggie's father, gave him her best wide-eyed look. Her gown's tiny spaghetti straps fought a losing battle to hold up the daringly low-cut bodice, and her breasts quivered with each syllable she spoke. Next to her, Con sat and tried not to stare, fearing her top would fall off one minute and hoping it would the next. Maggie watched him with a benign smile, not quite upset, not quite jealous.

"Penelope, alongside you, this crowd is as dowdy as a mud hen in a dusty field," the senator said.

At that, Penelope brought her slim hand to her mouth and cast her eyes downward, a young coquette if you didn't know her. "That's just political talk, Senator. I won't vote for you."

"That's true," said Steven Dye, taking her hand in his. "You *can't* vote until we make a citizen out of you. Now you're just a British mercenary, a hired gun from a failing empire. Nothing more than that."

She leaned forward, clutching Steven's hand, her breasts a mere breath away from complete exposure. "He's right, Senator. I don't mean that I *wouldn't* vote for you. I mean, I can't vote for you. I'm sure you're a perfectly good lord."

"Senator."

"Lords, senators, congressmen, the House of Commons. All the same, really. Don't you agree, Senator?" She leaned forward a short distance. The Senator's eyes shifted from her face to her breasts. As always, when anyone, male or female, looked at Penelope James's breasts, her nipples hardened. It was a sight to see.

Maggie, her face impish and flushed with champagne, said, "Father, whatever you do, don't ask this child a question she can't answer."

"Why is that, Mags?" Her father's gaze didn't waver.

"Because she just might shrug her shoulders if she doesn't know the answer."

Steven Dye jumped up and raised his glass. "A toast! To Penelope James and her shruggable shoulders!" The lean-bodied redhead, full of wine, leaned a bit as he stood, an arm outstretched toward Penelope, his glass somewhat unsteady in his hand. "Here, here!", said the usually silent Michael Burns. They all stood up, in a toast to Penelope's . . . to her breasts, apparently. Naturally enough, she joined in the toast herself.

"You yanks! You're just the cat's binkum!" The party was getting convivial as hell, but Con Duggan advised Maggie that he wasn't at all sure he wanted to be the "cat's binkum," whatever that was. . . .

11:45 P.M.

The senator turned the conversation to politics. "We don't get much response about anything from your people, Con. Truth is, even my committee has damn little idea what you do."

"Systems testing, most of the time, Senator."

"Call me 'Champ,' please, Con. And exactly what systems are you testing? Only a week ago, I told the President

I was unhappy with your accountability. Do you know what he said, Con?"

"Probably that we weren't responsible to anyone, particularly Senate committees."

"Damn right! His exact words! Well, I can tell you, I let him know that in no way would I allow you people to spend the kind of money I think you're spending without telling my committee where the hell it went!"

"But, the President didn't agree, did he, Daddy?"

"Champ" Stuart glared at his daughter, his only child, the source of so many contradictory emotions and upheavals in his life.

"No, he didn't. So I thought I'd just pop up here to this soiree of yours and invite myself out to see that base of yours. Nevada, isn't it? At Nellis?"

At this point Michael Barns took up the gauntlet. "We do have a small installation at Nellis Air Force Base, Senator . . . but I can't authorize a visit."

"Why not, Mr. Barns? It's your outfit."

"No, Senator, not mine. It's just in my care. We handle things that need handling with a minimum of fuss and political involvement. Only the President can authorize a visit. The unit is top secret, and security is vital to its continued effectiveness."

"Are you suggesting, sir, that a United States Senator of twenty years' service to his country is a risk?"

"I'm suggesting no such thing, Senator Stuart. I'm simply stating the President's policy. And it's my understanding that you and the President are not exactly close."

"Daddy, it's New Year's eve, and I want to forget the damned unit for a while. I see little enough of Con as it is," Maggie told him.

"Well, you could start the solution to that by moving out of that damn house in the wilderness. I don't understand your willingness to pack your ideals away like that!" Now the senator was genuinely indignant.

That attitude incited Penelope beyond her capacity to remain still. "Oh no, Senator! They couldn't do that! Steven and I spent a wonderful month there the summer past, and we're going again next year. She mustn't move. Oh, Maggie, tell him you'll not move from that lovely place. The bedroom's huge! Why, Steven and I stayed thirty-one hours in that room, and we . . ."

"Penelope!" There were limits to what Maggie would allow her precocious young friend to talk about.

"Oh, right. I do rattle on so. It's from me mum's side, Senator. She was once a fine lady, but she talked too much, just like I do."

"She must have been a lovely woman, Penelope."

"Oh, yes, Senator, she was. You might say she had more gentlemen callers than she could handle. But she did her best—to handle them, I mean."

The senator sensed that Penelope was toying with him, but he couldn't quite place how that had been done. "Do you see your mother often, Penelope?" he asked.

"Not since I was thirteen." Penelope tossed down her drink and held it out to Con to be refilled. The senator abandoned his line of questioning.

"They don't look like much." Karen Black, recruited for this mission less than a week before, sat next to Martin Brooks and posed like a glistening blond Barbie Doll come to life, her veins coursing with potent drugs supplied to her by the man who had essentially become her master. Picked up by Brooks and raped in the back of his limousine on Christmas Eve, she had been turned into a thrill-seeking, bloodthirsty adventuress in less than a week.

Peter Coy Booker had recruited and drugged most of the women who had worked for him over the past thirty years. The system was foolproof. He simply kept the ones he didn't kill first. This method had not changed for the "new" Booker. Martin Brooks, a year of convalescence and hatred behind him, operated the same way. If anything, he was even more criminally insane than he'd been before his last encounter with Con Duggan and his team.

"Oh, but they *are* my dear. Very much, indeed. Mr. Duggan and the young man and woman blew up my boat, stopped an operation before I could start it, and killed or arrested all my best operatives in England. But you're going to start their downfall right here, tonight."

"Just by getting the older bitch to go to the bloody ladies' room?"

"Exactly. That, for tonight, is your only job."

"Then what?"

Martin Brooks gave her a cold, waxen-faced stare. "Miss Black, if you accomplish your simple duties, I shall buy you a new Porsche. If not, I shall take . . . some other action." Booker, in the year he'd spent in Highgate Hospital, had changed in every physical way. Even his accent, once heavy with an Australian lilt, had disappeared, replaced by a smooth, non-accented flow. What had not changed were his eyes and what they conveyed. Miss Black knew instinctively what he meant by "some other action."

"When I give you the signal, excuse yourself, and ask Miss Stuart to accompany you to the lounge, just as we practiced. Do that, and all will be well. Now, let's you and I just invite ourselves to their little party, shall we?"

Frightened but excited as well, Karen Black, wearing a $7,500 Galanos dress, accompanied her new master across the twenty feet of ballroom floor separating the two tables. She looked every inch a lady gone a bit trampy with money. That was partly true, but she'd never been a lady.

The senator was a Democrat with a history of switching sides. Karen Black had huge breasts and a willingness to expose them. Penelope had nice breasts, "just right," she called them, but they were small potatoes compared to Karen's. When Karen Black was introduced, the senator found a chair for her next to him. She immediately gave him her undivided attention.

"Have we met, Mr. . . . ?" Here Con Duggan glanced down at the card delivered to their table with the champagne.

"Brooks, Mr. Duggan. Martin Brooks."

For a brief instant, Con Duggan heard, or thought he heard, another voice, not Martin Brook's; somebody, someplace . . .

"We've never met formally, as it were. But we met once years ago, at a New South Wales open combat pistol shoot."

" '84, wasn't it?" Con knew it wasn't '84. He hadn't shot anywhere in competition that year.

" '82, actually. You shot third overall, if I recall. And I do. I'm a bit of a fuss-budget about details."

The echo, the second, past voice, disappeared, if it had ever been there, before Con could recognize that he was sitting face to face with a man he thought was quite unable to speak, being dead and all.

"And you, Mr. Brooks . . ."

"Martin, please. I'm not a formal person. 'Mister' implies one person is better than someone else, my father said. I hold the same view."

"Okay. Martin it is. In '82, in New South Wales, where did you place?"

"Ah. Well, regrettably, I had just recently suffered an accident." Here Booker held up his leather hand. "I stopped active competition in 1980, the Steel Challenge in Missouri. An SOF Convention."

"Then, if I may ask, what brought you to a minor championship in New South?"

"Guns and those who use them. I'm a designer of weapons. They are both my work and my hobby. Participating in firearms competitions, even as a spectator, satisfies some of my longing to shoot. I designed the Hart .45 that won that competition in 1980."

"Oh, really? The word on the circuit was Peter Coy Booker designed the Hart .45."

"Booker? No truth to it. I designed it, but he bought the early drawings and claimed it for his own. Still, *I* designed the weapon. He paid me too much to worry about whose name is on the patent."

The two men were talking as if the thousand or so people in the ballroom for the New Year's festivities were not there, or were silent, painted characters illustrated to form a backdrop for the new play they were collaborating on. Maggie had been observing the two of them, and a look of inexplicable apprehension and foreboding shadowed her face.

"Con, are you going to introduce me to this exquisite creature at you side?" she finally asked.

"Oh! Well, sure; Maggie Stuart, this is Martin Brooks, buyer of champagne for tables full of strangers."

"How better to break the ice?" She smiled, the shadows gone from view. At that moment, as happened often in their relationship, Con found himself grateful beyond belief that she loved him. She had taken his life from his shaky hands long ago and rebuilt it with a passionate resolve to succeed. He was what he was because of her unfailing faith in what she used to call "stuff that's just meant to be."

"How kind of you, Maggie. May I call you Maggie?"

"Don't know why not. I intend to call you Martin. Hell, I'm drinking your champagne, which, where I come from, means whatever you want it to mean. It means that tonight is New Year's Eve. I've had my man with me for the better part of a year, and I hope for a quiet new one as well."

"From your remarks, Maggie, I assume Con is gone for various lengths of time. I consider that criminal behavior, if true."

"Actually, Martin," replied Con, "I'm practically a stick in the mud. We live quietly up in Alaska. I do some government consulting to keep my hand in, so to speak. Out in the desert. Tanks and stuff. I only shoot competitively in the major meets now. All the hotshot teeny-boppers, like Mr. Dye here, can outshoot me."

"Mr. Dye?"

Steven spun around in his chair and stuck his hand out. "Did someone call my name?" Martin Brooks took Steven Dye's hand with his good one.

"Mr. Martin Brooks, may I introduce you to two of my less reverent associates. Steven Dye, weaponeer, and Penelope James."

"Weapon! That's what I am," Penelope giggled. "And a bloody cute one, at that. How d'ya do."

"Penelope is, how should I say, in her cups," Con said.

"Not either. In *his* cups." Penelope's hand disappeared

beneath the table, and Steven Dye jumped but otherwise remained comparatively calm.

"You both need to go home."

"Ol' Con Duggan. Wise old Con Duggan. Mr. Martin Brooks, I've seen your eyes before—somewhere. But another man was usin' 'em at the time. Blew hisself up in the Channel, boat and all, and now you got his eyes. I'm drunk and terrorizing the colonies tonight, as any proper English woman should do." With that, she turned toward Karen Black and shrieked with glee when she discovered she was sharing the table with a fellow countryman. "She's bloody British, hey everybody, lil' Miss Black here is a flamin' drunkin' Brit. Well, she might not be drunk yet, but we'll work on it. Tell me, you trixie little thing, just where in the east end were you born?"

"Steven?" Duggan interrupted.

"Yeh, Con."

"Right after midnight, you take her back to the hotel room before she starts a revolution."

"Yes, sir," said a subdued Steven Dye.

"Dispensing wisdom, Con?" Martin Brooks asked with a hint of irony.

"Yeah, well, at my age, that's pretty much all I'm allowed to dispense. Somehow white hair is equated with wisdom. Bullshit, of course, but my young friends expect it of me."

"An interesting group at this table, Con. One wonders what, exactly, makes people of such disparate origins and places a unit."

"Unit? We're friends, that's all. The senator, so mesmerized by your buxom companion, is Maggie's father. I assumed he was the main reason for your interest in this table."

"Mr. Dye designs weapons systems, does he not?"

"Sure. What I do and what he does throws us together a lot. We're good friends. Keep them away from the champagne, and they're good company as well."

"I'm sure they are, and I hope to see you all under less, how shall I put it, frivolous circumstances."

"Sure. I'll be in touch."

"Well, only a few minutes until midnight." He pressed a button on the back of his leather hand, and, on the street below, the kidnap team moved into action.

The band on Chin K. Lee's right wrist began to blink as Booker sent the signal to act. They had somewhere between five and eight minutes to get to the hallway that encircled the ballroom. Chin motioned to his companions, and they exited the van after activating the emergency lights on the roof. They pulled the stretcher from the rear, and Chin carried a small medical bag. It contained hypos and sedatives for their "patient." The "plan," such as it was, was no more than a quick snatch and grab. Not very sophisticated, but if all went as planned, effective enough.

"It's almost midnight, and I have to visit the ladies' room, but I haven't the foggiest idea where it is." Karen Black gave the senator a most appealing smile.

"C'mon, you trixie little thing. I'll take you, but God and you and I know you're no lady," Penelope said with a slight slur. She stood up, tottered on her heels, and flopped back down into her seat. "Bloody 'eels. Not meant to be worn outside of bed because one can't walk properly in them. I fuck properly in them, but I can't seem to walk very well."

"Maggie, would you accompany my friend to the ladies' room? I fear she's a bit tight," Martin said, concern oozing from his voice.

"They're both a bit more than tight. Of course I'll take her. We have just enough time to go and be back for Auld Lang Syne and a bright new year. Hold those lips, old Con Duggan, your fair maid will return. C'mon, child, let's explore the highways and byways of this great hall."

Maggie Stuart, in her forties, still commanded attention, and many an admiring glance followed the two women as they made their way across the ballroom. The tall elegant brunette, the white streak of hair that ran full length through the black adding to her glamour, and the overly lush blonde, bordering on chubby but blatantly sexual, created a ripple of sensation as they moved through the crowded tables.

"You don't deserve her, Duggan. She's too good for you," Brooks said.

Con turned to look at Martin Brooks, fixing on his eyes. Familiar. Hard, now. "You're absolutely correct, Martin. I don't deserve her. Nobody knows that better than I."

Nobody paid much attention to the white-coated attendants as they rushed across the lower lobby, commandeering with ease a full elevator, the passengers eager to help in the "emergency." They rode the elevator straight to the ballroom floor and locked it in the stop position. The back hallways were nearly empty this close to midnight. Chin watched as his target, escorted by Karen Black, disappeared into the ladies' room. The three "medics" glanced into the ballroom, but no one seemed to be paying any attention to them. A tall, dignified-looking man was headed their way. The three men continued down the hall, stopping outside the ladies' room.

"He's a looker, that old man of yours."

"Do you think so, Miss Black?"

"Oh, yeah. Bet he knows a bit, that one."

Maggie took one last look at herself in the mirror, trying to stay with this odd, personal conversation with the decidedly strange Miss Black. The blonde, standing in the same mirror space, had flushed cheekbones and was shifting from foot to foot nervously, a kind of St. Vitas dance.

"Are you all right, dear?" Maggie addressed Karen Black as if she were a child. At that moment the door burst open, and three men dressed in white entered the lounge, pulling a stretcher toward the two women.

"Who are you? You can't just walk in here like this! There's nobody here in need of your services!" Maggie was livid with indignation.

Chin didn't answer her but strode to her side, grabbed her, and applied an ancient martial arts technique to a nerve in her shoulder. She tried to scream, but couldn't. She couldn't move. The smaller of the two other men approached her, carrying a small bag. It was only then that Maggie began to fully realize what was happening to her. The man tore the wrapper off a hypodermic needle, inserted the tip into a small bottle, filled it, and popped the needle into her arm, all in one fluid motion. The room began to spin in, what seemed to Maggie, a slow, spiralling motion, and she fell into Chin's arms, aware of nothing.

Gently, he put her on the wheeled stretcher and covered her with a blanket. The team had neglected to do one small thing. Close the ladies' lounge door. Champ Stuart, United States Senator, Presidential hopeful, or at least wannabe, stood in the doorway, a little shaky on his feet. But he wasn't too far gone to recognize first Karen Black, identifying her breasts with a leering glance from his bloodshot eyes, and finally noticing the long black hair of his daughter as she was strapped onto the gurney.

"See here, that's my daughter, and just what the hell is going on? Who are you? Karen, what happened to Maggie?"

But Karen Black's only job had been to get Maggie in or near the ladies' room. She had no clever retort for Champ Stuart. "She, ah, she just passed out, so I called for help, and these gentlemen came."

"You, sir! Where do you think you're taking her? I'm her father and I want to—"

Chin nodded once, and the same drug that flowed in Maggie's veins was jammed into the Senator's thigh. The two men caught him before he hit the floor.

"What do we do with him?" one of them asked.

Chin thought about it, but not for long. It was two minutes to midnight. He undid Maggie's straps and picked her up from the stretcher, handling her weight easily.

"Him first," Chin directed.

The senator took Maggie's place on the bed and was covered by a blanket. Chin placed Maggie's unconscious body on top and then strapped them both down. The trip to the elevator was uneventful. As the clock struck midnight, the now-loaded van pulled away, sirens wailing and lights blazing. The plan had worked. Too well. Peter Coy

Booker had managed to kidnap his chosen victim, Maggie Stuart. The senator was a problem, and this was relayed to Booker's earphone immediately. When asked for orders, he simply replied, "Proceed as planned." He'd figure out the complications later. At the moment, surrounded by drunken celebrants entering a new year, he felt more powerful than at any other time in his life.

He looked at Con's worried face. He, Martin Brooks, a.k.a. Peter Coy Booker, had returned. Let the game begin. He controlled the rules.

2

High Gate Surgical Hospital
July, 1993

"Now, Mr. Brooks, I don't want you to touch your face after I remove this final layer of post-operative wrap. You may look at it as closely as you wish, but it's a brand new face, fresh as a newborn. The skin must get acclimated before you go poking at it."

"Get on with it, Doctor." One by one, the gauze layers encircling his head were peeled away until Peter Coy Booker was free to look at his "new" face. It was a handsome face, which surprised him somewhat. The skin was very tight, a younger man's skin, nearly transparent with newness.

"Nicely done," Booker told his doctor.

"I'm glad you approve."

"What about the eyes?"

"The eyes, I'm afraid, remain yours exclusively. They're the mirror of your soul, like all eyes. You can disguise them with a variety of contacts. I could make some up."

"Do that. I have a dark soul, and I think it shows through even this new, impressive face of mine."

"Fine then. I'll have them made up. You have perfect eyesight, so their only function will be cosmetic."

"What the bloody hell, Doc. I'm cosmetic from head to toe."

"Yes, I guess you are at that. What color would you like your hair to be?"

15

"What? Oh . . . leave it blond. It suits me, somehow."

"You know, Mr. Brooks, your own mother wouldn't rec-ognize you now. Whatever you wanted to hide, and why, I don't know, but you're no longer who you were."

Wrong, of course. As Martin Brooks, Peter Coy Booker was worse than ever.

The ballroom erupted with songs, balloons, noisemakers, and confederate yelps. Couples kissed, strangers kissed, and Penelope and Steven Dye were doing something a little more akin to vertical oral sex. As 1993 shifted into the new year, Con Duggan's anxiety grew apace. He knew something was wrong, he felt it. The air in the ballroom seemed to have thinned, and he found himself short of breath.

"The ladies seem to have been caught up in the festiv-ities," Brooks said.

"Yeah, Martin, it's beginning to look that way. Not like Maggie to do this."

"Con?" Michael Barns was leaning across the table to speak to him.

"Happy New Year, Michael," Con replied without even a trace of mirth.

"Same to you. Where's Mags? I want to smooch that girl, and New Year's Eve is the only chance I get each year."

"Lost in the crowd, momentarily. But I'll give her the message."

"Look at those two! Better throw some cold water on them before he spreads her out right here on the table."

Michael was exaggerating, but not much. Penelope was standing on one high-heeled foot, her other leg wrapped around Steven Dye's upper calf, her incredible ass rolling against his groin as if they were alone in the room.

"Too late, Michael. Water won't help."

Michael Barns had seen them together before, but not the completely uninhibited display he now saw.

The young couple clutched each other, Steven trying to hold her hips still while she gripped the back of his belt with long-nailed fingers, pulling him tighter against her body. Sweat beaded their foreheads and trickled down the shadowed canyon between her breasts.

"Look at that. Dry humping to climax in the Carlton Ballroom." Con Duggan was actually embarrassed by their behavior.

"Can you die from too much sex?" asked Michael.

Con laughed and cast an anxious glance the length of the room, focusing on the arched entryway he'd last seen Maggie and her tipsy blond friend walk through. Last year—they'd gone through that doorway last year. . . . "If it's possible to die from too much sex, Steven Dye would already be dead."

Penelope James clung to Steven Dye, her body shaking from the aftershocks, her smile wide, happy, and real. Steven Dye looked dazed, happy, and flushed with too much champagne.

"Con?" It was Michael Barns again. "Something's wrong here."

"Feels like it," Con agreed.

"Let's go find Mags. She'll miss the whole year."

"Good idea. Will you excuse us, Martin? We seem to have misplaced the ladies."

"Of course, Mr. Duggan. Be my guest. I shall hold down the fort and put some shrimp on the barbie."

"Yah. You do that. C'mon, Michael." Somewhere in the dark past, he could hear Peter Coy Booker's voice saying, *"Not to worry, Duggan. When you crawl out of the native-infested jungle with another notch on your ancient weapon, I'll be right here with some shrimp on the barbie."*

The two men pushed their way through the celebrants, bumping, getting bumped, and occasionally kissed by strange women. Con's face was set hard, his sniper eyes working, trying to sort out and separate all the faces framed in his mind's eye, photographed, scanned, rejected. When they reached the women's lounge area, they discovered the hall was crammed to its gilded walls with expensively gowned, impatient arbiters of society, all needing to relieve their bladders at the same time. Con was absolutely certain she wasn't behind the polished wooden door with LADIES scripted in gold paint.

"Let's go get Penelope. She can check inside," Con said.

"Ya know, Con, even if she's not inside, we really have nothing to worry about. Her father's gone too. He's probably got her cornered somewhere, trying to get her to throw you out of her life."

"Oh, swell. Michael, this is no time for good sense. Maggie would never kick me out on New Year's Eve."

"Yeah. You're probably right. Let's go find the divine Miss Penelope James. She can be our bird dog."

The fight back through the crowded ballroom was worse than the trip out to the ladies' room. Everybody had stopped, or at least postponed, kissing-in the new year. Now they were crowded against each other, intending to dance the night away. The Confirmed Kill Team's table was empty. Even Martin Brooks had disappeared. The two men sat down and poured themselves a drink. The champagne had gone flat.

"Do you see the kids?" asked Michael Barns. To him, Steven and Penelope were "the kids."

"Nope. They're out in that crowd somewhere. We could yell 'fire.' Penelope would grab Steven and bounce right over everybody's head. Steven calls her Wonder Woman."

"She is, in her own little disorderly way. But they're still both kids. I wonder where our self-introduced friend went." Michael looked briefly around the room.

"Mr. Martin Brooks? Probably off to more fertile pastures. Maggie's gone, the senator's gone, and, so it seems, is little Miss Karen Black. That thought just occurred to me. Find her or Maggie's dad, and we'll probably find them all. Still, I'm not comfortable with any of this."

"Feels like a hot LZ doesn't it, Con?"

"Just like one. Any minute now, we'll be taking incoming."

"Mr. Duggan?" A man in a tuxedo with a hotel nameplate identifying him as "John" stood next to the table, hands behind his back.

"That's me, pal."

"I have a note for you, sir." His hand appeared from behind his back, and he extended a small white envelope to Con, who took it and asked, "Who gave you this?"

"A man, sir. A guest, apparently. He didn't give his name, and I didn't ask." As Con reached for his money, the young man said, "Thank you, sir, but it's been taken care of."

"He tipped you?"

"He did, sir. Handsomely."

"No doubt. I'll get back to you if you're around and I need to reply."

"The gentleman suggested he was sure you would reply, but not by note."

"I see. Was he alone?"

"He was, sir, if you don't count the bodyguards. They didn't speak to him, nor he to them, but he had four very large men with him."

"When did he give you this note?"

"At midnight, sir. Forty minutes ago."

"Thank you."

"Yes, sir." John was the kind of slimy hotel employee Con liked. If paid enough, in coin or flattery or degree of obeisance, they were useful sources of information. He stared at the white envelope, tapping it rapidly against the table.

"You gonna open that, Con?" Michael asked.

Con opened the envelope, read the note, and slid it across the table.

"So what does it mean, exactly?"

"It means you were right. This is a hot LZ And that little note is definitely incoming."

The note was brief:

> *Dear Mr. Duggan:*
> *Shrimps on the barbie,*
> *with guests on the way.*
> *Join us, why don't you?*
> *Martin Brooks*

Penelope swept out of the ladies' lounge, her short dress flaring around her hips as she walked toward the waiting men. She walked directly to Con Duggan and took his hands in hers. She opened her hand, palm up. A single diamond earring lay there, a bright arrow of precious stone, evidence that Maggie, and probably her father, had been abducted by person or persons unknown. Con Duggan couldn't prove what he thought and could hardly believe his thoughts.

"I talked to the maid. She doesn't remember Maggie or Karen Black, if that's her real name. I offered her a slight amount of cash for a bit more of what she may have seen. Turns out she saw medics with a stretcher, but she couldn't see much else. She found the earring a little while back, just inside the lounge door. It's Maggie's, isn't it, Con?"

"Yeah. It's Maggie's."

"Well, wot the bloody 'ell is going on here? Where's she gone?" When Penelope was excited, she reverted to East End slang, but she was working hard to lose her accent.

"Michael?" Con gave his nominal superior a hopeful look.

"I don't know. Somebody snatched her, but he wanted the senator. She just got in the way."

"I don't think so, Michael. I think the man who bought us the champagne took her. He had familiar eyes. He looked like . . . he looked like . . . Peter Coy Booker."

There. Now it was said. Out loud.

"Con, what are you saying?" Steven Dye wasn't sure he was following this line of thought.

"I'm saying, Steven, that Booker didn't die when the *Stingray* blew up. I'm saying that Mr. Brooks is Mr. Peter Coy Booker—after Frankenstein made him whole again. He's taken her somewhere, and he wants me, or all of us, to come after him. It's a sick game, a typical Booker game."

"I blew the *Stingray* into small pieces, Con. You saw it. We all saw it. Target down, confirmed kill."

"I don't care what we think we saw. I looked into Peter Coy Booker's eyes. Martin Brooks/Booker. Call him what you want. He has Maggie."

"Not to mention a United States Senator, Con."

"That, too, Michael. I doubt that Booker wanted him involved, but Maggie and Champ vanished from this room over an hour ago. I conclude that a kidnapping has taken place. We have to try to keep it quiet, if possible."

"Con, we have to tell the President," Michael said.

"Fine, but meanwhile, let's get ourselves ready. I have an idea all of this is going to move very fast when it breaks. Activate the 21A Team. Turn on the power. He'll get back to us, and soon. We have to be ready to take him on."

"The President may have other ideas, Con."

"Other ideas? Why? What?"

"A U.S. Senator. The President will want to use the Delta Unit. He agreed to give them a shot. We might be used, we might not."

"Michael?"

"Yeah, Duggan."

"You know I'll go after her, no matter who the authorized unit is. Delta Force will only get her killed."

"This will go public, Con. And it will, if you're correct, turn into a nasty little game, with Maggie at the head of the firing line. If we have no authorization to go, we can only watch."

"You don't believe that, do you Michael? Really?"

"Hell, no. I assume that we—at least the four of us—will go after him, authorized or not."

"Penelope?" Con asked.

"Of course!"

"Steven?"

"She's family, Con. We go."

"Okay. That's settled. We'll go through the motions with the President. Then we wing it."

"Booker . . . Bloody hell, how can this be true?" Penelope was close to tears.

Con studied Penelope's beautiful face, now shadowed in sadness and disbelief. He tried to answer her doubts. "It's true, all right. This is her earring. She left it for us. Booker's alive because he's thoroughly evil—that kind of evil has extra lives, like a cat. And he picked the one among us who is totally innocent of causing him any harm. He chose the one of us he knew would most push me to extremes, knowing you all would follow wherever I lead, to whatever end.

"He's changed his looks, his voice, taken away some of the rough edges of the gun-running, drug-trafficking crime king. This operation is not a 'for profit' deal, though he may ask our government to ante-up some cash for the good senator. For Maggie, he wants terror. He wants to play with her and let me know about it.

"In the end, he'll tire of the game and want to end it. That's when he'll tell us to come to him. On *his* terms! If we do that, I think we'll all be killed. So we've got to make plans for him—find him first, kill him first. Then we reunite my Mags with her lost earring. . . ."

Penelope looked deep into Con Duggan's eyes. What she saw in their depths was a sure death sentence for Martin Brooks, a.k.a. Peter Coy Booker.

3

Maggie struggled to open her eyes, and a sharp pain shot
from the top of her head to her shoulders. Bright, harsh light
seemed to sweep across her face until she realized she was
blindfolded with a soft, diaper-like material tied at the back
of her head. She looked down under the blindfold and saw a
bright red carpet. She tried to move her arm and discovered
her arms were tied to what felt like an airliner seat. The
flashes of light, she would later find out, were caused by
aircraft landing lights on a nearby taxiway that swept her
window as the planes turned onto the main runway.

Booker had not had to change the "B" part of the logo on
the tail of the small, ten-seat corporate jet. The sleek white
aircraft had had the letter "M" added, so "MB" decorated
the tail in gaudy red and black.

Inside, Maggie began to twist her head from side to side
and tried to remove the blindfold by rubbing her cheek
against her shoulder. She smelled a flowery perfume, then
soft hands at the back of her head, and finally she could
see. She was, indeed, tied to a chair on an airplane. A few
feet away sat her father, not yet awake.

"So, Maggie, you've chosen to join the party. Bloody
exciting, don't you think? By the way, happy new year."
Karen Black, comfortably dressed in running shorts and
a T-shirt, gave her a cheerful smile even though she was

23

obviously drunk, or on drugs, or both. "He said he'd get ya, and he did!"

"Who? Who got me?"

"Peter Coy Booker."

"That's insane, Karen. Con Duggan killed Booker. He told me he did. In the harbor, at Folkestone, England. Booker's dead."

"Nope. He's just calling himself Brooks now. I get a new Porsche for delivering you to the ladies' room."

"What about my father?"

"Him? The old bloke is fine. Sleeping like a babe."

"Why us? Why me?"

"You. Just you. We weren't supposed to take nobody but you. The senator just sort of fell in with the wrong crowd. Funny. That's a funny joke. Is he really a senator, Maggie Stuart?"

"Yes, he really is."

"Well, Mr. Brooks will think of something to do with him."

"Let him go—that would be the best thing to do."

"Oh no. Shame on you, trying to influence an innocent girl to do wrong. Clear your head, Maggie. We won't be here very long. We're going to the beach. I even have a suitable bikini for you to wear while we wait."

"Wait? Wait for what, Miss Black?"

"Karen."

"Oh, all right. Karen. What are we waiting for?"

"For your hero, Maggie."

"Con?"

"Right. He comes to rescue you—Booker kills him. Tidy, don't you think?"

Maggie tried without much success to piece together what was happening. If what Karen Black had said was true, she and her father were in a frightening predicament. Maggie wasn't supposed to be privy to the many and varied secrets of the Confirmed Kill Team's missions. But snuggled in the warmth of her arms, trusting her completely, Con had, to the best of her knowledge, told her all about the first two missions of the team. The last mission, to attack the bullet train in Japan to topple a Japanese gangster kingpin, had been hairy and full of unexpected events. But as far as she knew, it was regarded as a successful team mission.

She knew even more about the first mission, the assassination of a world-wide terrorist leader, responsible for drug and weapons shipments, and the direct and indirect cause of thousands of deaths worldwide. Only after the mission, in fact not until months had passed since the *Stingray* had blown up, had Con opened up to her. Not so much about the mission to England itself. Much of that seemed to her inexplicable, impossible, and fantastic, even though Con admitted to very few of the "hellacious details," as Steven Dye called them.

The most startling aspect of that mission had been the saga of Penelope James becoming a trusted member of the team, though the young woman seemed to be not only immature and oversexed, but also screwed on a bit too tightly for most people to deal with. But she had stuck: Penelope was in love with Steven Dye, and she worshipped Con Duggan, her father-figure come to life. She treated Maggie with good-natured, female banter that never crossed the line of genuine respect. The Confirmed Kill Team was her family.

Booker had been a lifelong adversary for Con and had been the bait the government used to bring the veteran shooter on board and back into the shadowy government service he was best suited for. Killing Booker had been government-ordered. But to Con Duggan, it was clearly a matter of personal honor, the settling of an old debt. The final operation to expiate two decades of psychic pain.

Now, it seemed, came a new, terror-filled truth. Peter Coy Booker was not, in fact, dead. And under the guise of Martin Brooks, he had returned to kill his would-be killer. Maggie was bait, and she knew Con would move heaven and earth to save her life. She was the damsel in distress, Con the man on the white steed. She had to think, to watch, to learn all she could about her situation and her captors. If it was true that her father was not intended to be part of this, the Booker Plan was already seriously astray. Would that make her plight, Con's plight, the team's plight, more or less dangerous? And if what Booker sought was the death of his enemy, would it matter?

She resolved to remain calm and to sow disunion and untruth wherever possible among Booker and his cohorts. Con would be coming, somehow. She must be prepared when that time arrived. She was Con Duggan's woman. She'd do what was expected of her; she was prepared to die for her lover. Nothing else held sway. Even tied to a plush aircraft seat, she began plotting to kill Martin Brooks/Booker. There were no limits to what she might do. If Booker had a weakness, she'd exploit it. She chuckled.

Karen Black looked up from her solitaire game. "Something funny, love?"

"Yes. I was just thinking about a cartoon I used to really like."

"Oh, I love cartoons!"

"Do you remember the Tasmanian Devil? The one that had sharp teeth and short spiky hair and went whirling from place to place, wreaking havoc on everything in its path? A kind of toothy whirlwind?"

"No, don't think I've seen that one. Good, was it?"

"Oh, no. Bad. The Tasmanian Devil was very bad. You'll see."

"I beg your pardon?" Karen gave Maggie the quizzical look of a child.

"Nothing, Miss Black. Nothing at all. . . ."

The senator woke up just as the Lear jet cleared the runway and headed southeast. After the jet had pulled itself into the air, Maggie was freed from her bonds and allowed to walk about the cabin. Four expressionless orientals, led by Chin K. Lee, sat near the cabin door. She had not seen the pilot.

"Put these on, Maggie Stuart. No dresses where we're going." Karen Black handed her a pair of shorts and a scooped-neck top.

"Here?"

"Yes, here. Just put them on. The sandals, too. Don't worry about the guys seeing your body. Where we're going, they'll likely see a lot more of it."

Maggie looked at the men, then back at Karen Black. Well. So this was to be a game too? She unbuttoned her party dress and kicked off her dressy high heels. Next went her bra and pantyhose. She slipped into the wispy beach shorts and pulled the lime-colored silk blouse over her head, letting it drop over her breasts without the slightest show of discomfort. She would give these slimy little men everything and nothing at the same time. The sandals went on last, the straps weaving sexily up her ankles.

"Did you pick these, Karen?"

"Who, me? Lands, no. The man himself. He said he knew exactly what you'd like."

A brief survey showed a sleek blouse, too low-cut for modesty, silk shorts too high for her lush buttocks, and strappy sandals that directed attention to her naked legs. "Tell him he was right," Maggie said evenly.

"You can tell him yourself tomorrow, when he gets to the island."

"Island? What island?"

"Predator Bay, I think he calls it."

"Predator Bay. Sounds ominous."

"It's lovely. I've seen pictures. Ninety degrees every day and water so clear you can read a book thirty feet down."

"You sound like a travel agent, Karen."

"Well then, I sort of am one, aren't I?"

"Okay, agent, can you tell me just where the hell Predator Bay is?"

"The tropics. That's all I know."

Her father had regained consciousness by this point. Like the politician he was, he woke up talking. He watched Karen toss Maggie's evening clothes into a gym bag and return Maggie another, newer one. Incredibly, it had Maggie's name on it in gold lettering.

"Clothes for every occasion, Maggie. The man bought them last summer."

"Sure of himself, wasn't he?"

"And why not? And you, Senator, how are you feeling after your shot? Hey, you stayed down and out for a long time."

"Time . . . what time is it?"

Karen looked at a slim gold band on her wrist. She was in the midst of changing her top, and the gold one she'd chosen was hanging around her neck. Idly stroking her nipple, breasts exposed, she glanced at the watch again.

"Three forty A.M., January the first. A new year, honey." She partially recovered her breasts but left all but one button on the blouse open. Maggie tried, with considerable difficulty, not to laugh out loud. She didn't know whether to feel sorry for the woman or spank her.

"Three forty." Champ Stuart's eyes remained on the exposed breast that Karen continued to stroke even after she sat down opposite them.

"Yup. You been sleepy-time for almost four hours. I like sex when I wake up, Senator. How about you?"

Maggie watched her dignified-looking, senator-father incredulously as he turned into a leering old man who seemed to have no idea his life was in danger.

"Papa, we're captives, and your behavior is disgusting. This girl you're turning on the charm for may very well be your killer. How Mama put up with your sick need for women, any woman, anytime, is beyond me." She didn't raise her voice. She spoke in the sad, resigned way of a disappointed child who once had been able to love and respect him, but who now felt only pity.

"I'm sorry, Maggie. I'm a bit groggy. My thoughts are hard to hold together. Who kidnapped me?"

"Me, Father. They brought you along because you stumbled in on them. I'm sure with hindsight, they'd like to send you back."

"Don't worry, Maggie. Why, hell, I'm a United States Senator! The Delta Force itself will be used to rescue us."

"The Army?"

"No, a mix. Good boys. I'm sort of the 'Patron Saint of Finances and Congressional Clout.' Their commander is Major General Barton Cassidy. A hell of a man. You've heard me speak of him."

"Oh, yes, Father. The one you've never stopped trying to set me up with."

"Well, that boy is like a son to me. A hero, too. His men worship him. This is just the kind of situation we can use to prove that the Delta Force is urgently required for our national security. Well, by God, whoever is behind this is in serious trouble, I can assure you. My colleagues were going to vote to cut the force. Now they'll see!"

"Is that how you view this, Father? A nice little test for your pet project on the Senate Armed Forces Committee?"

"It can't hurt."

"You don't know the man responsible for this."

"And you do? How?"

"If our sexy little Miss Black knows what she's talking about, Peter Coy Booker has come back from the dead with a new face, a new name, and a very old hatred."

"For you? Why? Who is this Booker fellow?"

"An old antagonist of Con's. Way back, early in Viet Nam, and even before. Last year, the President authorized his termination. Con was asked to do it and thought he had, but apparently Booker didn't die in the boat explosion Con's team rigged for him. And now, he's back to get Con, get to him through me. He was the man at our table in the hotel ballroom, the one you ignored in favor of Miss Black and her matched pair of tits. He said his name was Martin Brooks, and perhaps it is now, but his real name is Peter Coy Booker. New flesh, but the same old hatreds."

"I don't understand, Maggie."

"We'll talk more later. Right now I'm going to rest. These next few days are going to be the worst of our lives, and we're going to have to fight like hell just to survive. First and foremost, Father, you've got to keep that thought uppermost in your mind. We're fighting for our lives. But Con will save us. He'll kill Peter Coy Booker, this time up close and personal."

"But he won't, Maggie. I recently got the Presidential go-ahead for the Delta force to intervene in political kidnapings.

Like it or not, you'll see Barton Cassidy, not Con Duggan. And to that, I say *a-men*. You've wasted your life on that man, and now he's put you in this vulnerable position. But don't worry. Just be calm, and remember, I have considerable influence. I'm a U.S. Senator. They don't dare hurt us. This is just the kind of thing the general lives for."

There was little Maggie could think of in response. Basically, her father had told her she had bad taste in men, senators were powerful, and the Delta Force would save the day.

"Father, you've been in the Senate too long. If we get out of this, I think you should retire. Think about it. Now entertain Miss England here—I'm going to take a nap."

4

"So, Michael, you believe your Mr. Booker has returned from the dead, so to speak."

"Yes, Mr. President."

"And this Booker guy is back with a new face, a new name, and has just snatched a United States Senator from a crowded ballroom, and nobody saw it happen—is that right?"

"Essentially, yes, Mr. President. He was sitting at our table until the senator's daughter and his accomplice, Karen Black, went to the ladies' lounge in the hallway behind the ballroom. There, somehow, they were kidnapped. We've interviewed a number of people who recall an emergency vehicle, an ambulance, parked outside a service entrance prior to midnight. We checked it out, Mr. President. No ambulance or emergency vehicle had been dispatched in that time period to anywhere near the hotel. The hotel management told us that if it had been legit, it would have parked on the opposite side of the hotel."

"Your conclusion, Mr. Duggan?" the President asked.

"The senator and his daughter were taken from the fifteenth-floor lounge area using the hotel's regular elevators to get to the ground floor. Then they were loaded aboard a van and driven away."

"Where?"

31

"As yet, Mr. President, we have no idea."

"So, Michael, what's your plan? I can't sit on this. The papers will have to be told the truth—without all the details, of course."

"Sir, our plan for a rescue mission depends on Booker," Con said.

"I beg your pardon?"

"Mr. President, it's our belief that Peter Coy Booker didn't intend to take the senator," Michael told him. "Somehow, while the snatch was on, he showed up, and they decided, or were forced by something he said or did, to take him along as well."

"If they weren't after the senator, then who *did* they want?"

"Maggie Stuart, his daughter."

"I'm afraid I don't understand, Michael."

"Maggie and Con have lived together in Alaska for the past eighteen years. This assault on Maggie, we believe, is designed to suck the 21A Team into a no-win situation, using her as bait—get us where they want us and destroy the team. Booker wants Con dead, but first, as always, he's got to play his game. Our plan is to find him first, take him on our own terms, and free the hostages. All our resources are operating at full strength worldwide right now. The 21A base at Nellis is fully staffed. All systems are operating."

"Fine, Michael, fine. But when the hostages are located, you will stand down." The President's face was stern and gray—his Commander-in-Chief face.

"Sir? I don't understand."

"General Barton Cassidy and the Delta Force will be used in this operation. I can't allow you . . . and . . . you and Mr. Duggan here to ride-'em-cowboy after Miss Stuart. Delta Force is fully trained for an armed assault in hostage situations. This unit costs this government a billion dollars a year, and it's a pet project of Champ Stuart's. You have no evidence at this time to suggest a dead man came back with a new face, alive and prosperous, just to wreak havoc and revenge on Mr. Duggan by kidnapping his . . . his companion." The President had a strong, Calvinist streak in him. He didn't approve of "relationships" like Con and Maggie's.

"But, Mr. President, Michael and I know this man," Con protested, his agitation evident. "Way back in the sixties, in the Far East. I *thought* I saw him blown up in Folkestone Harbor, but somehow he lived through that, altered his appearance, and came after me."

"You mean, Miss Stuart," the President said.

"Same thing, Mr. President. He knew I'd come to get her."

"Sorry, Con. Cooperate with the general. Advise him, help him find his way. I want the senator to know that Delta Force will be there soon. They'll do the job. That's an order, you two. Don't go off half-cocked." He gave the two men his concerned-statesmen look.

Michael motioned Con to silence. His tone was even when he said, "Of course not, sir. If I were you, Mr. President, I'd leak, rather blatantly, that the senator's favorite unit will be involved. That'll give our Mr. Booker something to worry about."

"Thank you, Michael. You and Con have taken this very well, as I knew you would."

"It's our duty, sir. Good day, Mr. President, and happy new year."

"The same to you. Extend my best wishes to the 21A group on those first two missions. Marvelous, just marvelous!"

"Thank you, sir."

The two men were ushered from the Oval Office by the President's National Security Advisor. He gave them a moment of official sympathy. "Tough luck, guys. I want you to know I disagree with him. Delta Force couldn't find its asshole in a heat wave. But I just advise the President. In this case, he chose to ignore my advice. He's got the last word, of course."

"Thanks. Keep your peepers open and the wax out of your ears. Let us know if something interesting crosses your desk," Michael said.

"Now, Michael, you know I can't do that."

"Yeah, I know that. Still, we go way back. You owe me."

"Cheap shot."

"True. But, I'm a cheap-shot kind of guy."

"If I think you have a need to know something, I'll get it to you."

"Angels can't do more." They shook hands.

Outside the anteroom to the President's office, Michael and Con rejoined Steven Dye and Penelope James and walked four abreast down the long hallway. Penelope was dressed in a dressy short-skirted suit. Steven Dye wore a suit as well.

Penelope was the first to speak. "What did the President say, Con?"

"Penelope, he said we were out."

"Out! How the bloody hell . . . Damn it, this house should have stayed burned down when my British ancestors set fire to it."

"Penelope!" Steven admonished her.

"Sorry." But she wasn't.

"Who gets it?" Steven asked.

"Mr. Dye, the President has seen fit to hand this nasty business over to someone less emotionally involved," Con told him.

"Cassidy and the Delta Force?"

"Sad, but true. Oh my God, my poor Maggie." His teammates could hear the anguish in Con's voice. His face was stricken with fear for Maggie.

Penelope James walked a bit forward of the group and turned to face them. "Well, then, are we mutineers, or are we not?" She put her hands out, and the other three joined her in a childlike war huddle just inside the east entrance of the White House. "To mutiny, and to the absolute death of Peter Coy Booker!" Penelope chirped.

The 21A Confirmed Kill Team would now operate on its own, in secret. While its motives were honorable, its actions would be without the government's blessing. Delta Force had the job of rescuing Senator Stuart and his daughter—officially. Meanwhile, 21A began its mutinous conduct. They boarded the 21A C-130 and flew west to Nellis Air Force Base, the heart and soul of all

Confirmed Kill activities. As they cleared Washington, D.C. airspace, the President entertained the morning news shows with a press conference, activating the Delta Force on television. . . .

5

"Yes, Mr. President . . . Of course, sir . . . We'll find him, sir." Major General Barton Cassidy hung up the red secure phone, the one connected to the White House.

Finally. Delta Force would finally be used! Jesus Christ, the senator! Of all the people in the government to get himself snatched by some international bunch of crazies, Cassidy couldn't have picked the victim better if he'd done it himself.

The "Godfather Senator," Champ Stuart, the money man with the committee chairmanships, the man who kept Delta Force alive. Of course, the Force had been used in the Gulf war, but only on the broadest scale. They'd been extremely successful in penetrating and destroying enemy headquarters and radar facilities. In secret, of course. No publicity.

Now, by God, the President had come right out and mentioned Delta Force as a "possible" answer to the kidnapping. Privately, he, the President, had simply handed Delta Force the job and the authority to carry it out. God only knew what group had pulled it off.

Killings and kidnapings had become more of a problem internationally than ever before. Eastern Europe and the Soviet Republics were in a near constant state of civil

37

breakdown. Not war, exactly, but the next best thing. Christ, the head of the Croation League of the United States had been kidnapped, beaten, and hung from a church belfry while on a visit to England. IRA kidnapings and bombings, also mostly in England, were in focus. Japan was opening up, oozing corrupt power at every glistening corner, rotting from the inside while putting on a show of the new "morality of spirit," as they called it.

The world was fucked up for sure. And now he and a hand-picked force of hard-bitten, well-trained men had been ordered to step into the arena and play the game with the big boys. Well, he was ready.

The President had told him to keep in contact with some guy named Duggan out at Nellis. Nevada! What the fuck was in Nevada that he needed? Still, the President wanted him to talk to this guy. Where was the number? Here on his desk, somewhere. Fuck it. He was a general. If he pulled this off, his third star and the senator's everlasting gratitude were in the bag; his future would be assured.

He picked up the interoffice phone and asked his operation's man, a lieutenant colonel in the Marines, to get this Duggan on the line. Meanwhile, he ordered his various unit commanders to rendevous and assemble here, to make plans and get the show on the road. He expected to have the senator freed in forty-eight hours. That was his timetable. Now to talk to this Duggan guy. . . .

"I'm sorry, Colonel, but our commander is not on station at this time."

"What's his name again?"

"Duggan, sir."

"What's his rank?"

"Rank, sir? I don't know that he has one, although he's rated as a master sergeant, USMC."

"Master sergeant! Your commander is a master sergeant?"

"Not really, sir. He simply leads the group, whatever his rank."

"Well, I've been ordered by *my* commander to get this guy on the phone."

"He's airborne, sir. Would you like me to contact him aboard 21A?"

"What's 21A?"

"Everything is 21A, sir."

"Jesus Christ! Who am I talking to?"

"The duty operator for 21A channel. Now, Colonel, if you'll give me the proper coded sequence for today, I'll connect you with 21A, airborne over Texas at this time. Or if you wish, I can message the aircraft, and if he chooses, he'll call you. Or he may wait until he's back at Nellis. Mr. Duggan doesn't advise us where he's going to be. In fact, sir, I didn't expect him back on base, unless in an emergency, for two weeks."

"All right, lady, whatever you are. Hook me up to that guy airborne. This is Crosswind Commander, Delta Force."

"Do you have the number, sir?"

"What number? Goddamnit, I don't see why I'm being subjected to all this."

"Sorry, sir. But all 21A communications are monitored and recorded. We have to have the number to operate the system."

"Just what the hell do you people do out there?"

"I have no idea, sir. I operate a phone system."

"Do you know who I am, damnit?"

"Yes, sir. Your name is on my B-list."

"What the hell is a 'B' list?"

"No access without the daily code. Surely, sir, whoever asked you to call must have known that."

"Goddamn it, put me through!"

"I'm sorry, sir. This system will function automatically for the next fifteen seconds. Voice-activated by the proper code, it will select and connect you to the assigned number. These are standard procedures with 'A' priority, meaning 21A is in the activity mode. Those are my orders. In fifteen seconds, this cycle will shut down automatically. Have a good day, sir."

"Then the fucking system goes off, and I'm sitting out there like a Goddamn corporal, trying to get through to company headquarters. Christ, General, who is this guy and what the hell is 21A?"

"Settle down, Colonel. I'm not exactly sure what 21A is. It's listed as secret, and it has a lot of punch. Some kind of goofy think-tank, I hear, making wonder weapons or something."

"Rumor has it they're the bunch that took out the Jap on the bullet train."

"Japan denies it. An accident with only a few casualties. That's the story, anyway. And don't pay any attention to rumors. Hell, *Delta Force* couldn't have taken that train, so whoever 21A is, they *damn* sure didn't do it. By the way, here's the code number. Let's do it their way. Just get me this Duggan guy."

"Sergeant Duggan."

"That's a crock. Once, maybe, civilian now. But I don't give a shit what he is. If he can help us, I'll listen. If not, Delta can handle anything, right Bob?"

"Don't you, even for a minute, General, worry about this whole deal? I mean, we don't know how they vanished, why, with whom, or where. Right now they've just disappeared from the face of the earth."

"Well find 'em. We're Delta Force!"

"Of course, General. Still, let's add some muscle. Nevada communications handled me like a kid. You'd better use the code and those stars on your shoulder. Cut the tape and all."

"Yeah . . . Damned straight. I'm a fucking general, for Christ's sake. Gimme that phone. . . ."

"Will you hold please, General? We'll initiate contact with Mr. Duggan's aircraft. Thirty seconds, General."

"It's about time!" Like his assistant, and even with the proper codes, he'd been jerked around in ways he considered absolutely out of line. What the hell good were the two stars on his shoulder if they didn't open doors for him?

The phone whined, shifted to a steady beeping sound, then static crackled over the line. Finally, he heard it connect, and a voice sounding as if it were in the next room came on, a woman's voice.

"This is 21A–C-130, go Nellis," Penelope said.

"We have a clearance call for Mr. Duggan."

"Right-O, 21A. I'll just hop back and fetch him. He's cleaning a weapon at the moment, and I'm supposed to be bloody watching him do it. Wait one, 21A."

"Roger, 21A–C-130. General, you're on the hook. I'll leave you now. Mr. Duggan will pick up."

"Duggan here. How may I help you, General?"

"Well, Sergeant Duggan, if you'd start by making your communications system a little more accessible, why then . . ."

"Please get to the point, General. I know you've been assigned to the senator's kidnaping, so why don't I tell you what I know?"

"Okay. Tell me what you know."

"I know who snatched her."

"Her?"

"Maggie Stuart. The senator was an afterthought. He should be easy to get back. She won't be."

"How do you know these things?"

"Because Maggie Stuart and I share a life together, and we have for the past eighteen years. The guy who got them is officially dead, but less than twenty-four hours ago, he bought me a drink and we talked, but I didn't recognize him. Now I do. All the plastic surgery in the world can't alter those eyes. His are blue. He's six feet tall, one-seventy, with an athletic build. He has white-blond hair and he's about fifty. His resources are unlimited, and I don't believe you or the Delta Team will find him. I also believe that if you do, it'll result in the deaths of Maggie and her father. He took them to get me. You and Delta are a minor irritant. All you'll succeed in doing is muddying the waters and forcing him to move faster than he wants to. The pressure on the senator and Maggie Stuart will be very rough. Now, General, I want to ask you just one question. If you do locate them, are you willing to let me know so I can assist you?"

"Delta doesn't need help, and I have no idea what you people do, and I don't think I want to. But I'll be damned if I'll buy your cockamamie story about dead men buying drinks and stealing your girl."

"Are you saying you won't keep me informed, General?"

"Not in detail, no. I appreciate your emotional involvement, Mr. Duggan, and I'll keep in touch on that basis."

"It's your show, General. But we know this guy real well."

"I'm sorry, Duggan, but I just can't buy into that."

"Too bad. But it's your problem. I assume you know how to handle it."

"Of course I do."

"Bloody hell he will! What a twit!" Penelope's voice came clearly onto the line. "Con, this dinkum general will just get her killed." Penelope burst into audible tears.

"Duggan, who *is* that person? And why is she on a secure line? I demand to know!"

"She's on the line because she's a member of this team. She doesn't approve of you or your unit, and neither do I. You and I will just have to operate without each other's assistance, General."

"The President ordered you to stand down. I must insist that . . ."

"Goodbye, General. 21A–C-130 out."

Predator Bay, The Caribbean
8:00 A.M. January 1, 1994

The jet swung in a wide circle around the lush green island and its white sand beaches, then swooped low over the single-runway airstrip. It banked around the curious skull-shaped island, the tail of it a long dock with three boats tied up to it.

"Predator Bay?" Maggie said. Strapped in her chair, she watched as the jet sat down gently and rolled along the runway, turning off at an angle on a taxiway, its sleek white nose pointed at a cluster of white buildings with red tiled roofs, dominated by the central building of the group.

"Yes, though I haven't been here before. Martin has shown me pictures."

"What's going to happen to us, Karen?" Maggie's father asked.

"Don't know, Senator. I'm just along for the ride, you might say." Maggie watched Karen Black's face as the woman talked, looking for some sign of sisterhood. What she saw was anything but kinship. Karen was staring at Maggie's body, barely concealed by the bright lime low-scooped top and very tiny shorts.

The non-speaking, nearly invisible bodyguards, or prisoner warders, jumped into action as the plane rolled to a stop. They opened the passenger door, and the exit stairway hummed down electrically to the airstrip's surface. Two of the men went down the stairs, the cabin door leading to the flight deck opened, and a handsome pilot stepped into the passenger compartment. Right behind him, wearing cut-off jeans and a T-shirt, stood Martin Brooks, a strange demonic light in his eyes. He smiled as he gave his captives a cordial greeting. "Welcome to my little piece of paradise. Stay out of trouble and make no attempt to escape, and it will not be necessary to imprison you with all the distasteful images that word brings forth. You're my guests, although you, Senator, are not on my guest list. Chin will take you to your villa. It's small, but nice. You, Miss Stuart, may choose from the clothes hanging in your closets. You'll find everything you need. Please, view yourself as guests on one of the least-known islands in the Caribbean Sea. It's less than six miles around the island, four across it. You cannot get away. There's no way to escape, no place to hide, and we are two hundred miles off all normal lanes of commerce. You are my prisoners, of course, but this condition need not be painful."

"What are your plans for us, sir?"

"Senator, my plans are simple. You stay here until Con Duggan and his 21A Team arrives. Then we kill him, set you free, and take our leave. That, essentially, is the plan. Karen, you will share the larger guest villa with Miss Stuart. Dinner is at six P.M. Please, just follow your guide, but remember, they're not as stupid as they appear to be. If you try to escape, they are instructed to stop you by whatever means necessary. Now, if you'll forgive me, I'd like you all to join me near the plane on the tarmac. For a family picture, as it were."

He lined them up: Karen Black in her skimpy beach outfit, Maggie in blouse and short-shorts, her father still in a rumpled suit. The two women in the middle, her father on one end, Martin Brooks at the other. Just before one of the guards snapped the picture, Booker pulled Maggie's blouse off her breasts and fondled them. Frozen in terror, real terror, heightened and accentuated by the lushness and beauty of the island, Maggie could not move. Then he thrust his hand, the good one, down the front of her shorts and pulled savagely on her pubic hair. Maggie spun away as the camera whirred and clicked, and then she stood, trembling, and adjusted her blouse to cover her breast. Martin Brooks opened his palm, and small curly black hairs blew away on the tropic breeze.

"I imagine that will piss Con off, don't you think, Miss Stuart?" He turned away and headed along a brick sidewalk that seemed to go everywhere within the compound.

"Tell me, Maggie girl, whatever did your man *do* to Mr. Brooks?" the senator asked. Maggie glanced at her father. He hadn't moved. She didn't bother to respond to his question. With Karen Black at her side, a dead-faced pair of guards just yards away, she headed for her villa. This was going to be very, very bad. She tried not to think of the photo.

Seven hours later, in a sleepy Western Union office in the Caribbean, a man paid the fax fee, and in seconds, the set of pictures was on Michael Barns's desk. The originals were express-mailed to Michael and to the White House. Those sent to the White House showed the group before Booker's viciousness. Unharmed captives on one set, terror on the other.

6

"Oh, that horrid little man!" Penelope James had burst into tears when she'd first seen the pictures. "So bloody calculating, so bloody evil. Oh, I wish he were dead. Oh, Con, I want her safe. She . . . she's . . . well, she means such a great deal to me and all, and I look up to her. Sometimes we talk, oh, for hours, about things I can't talk to anybody else about, not even you, nor my lovely Steven yank. Oh, God, I'd rip his balls off! We blew up his boat! I saw it blow up. And now, now to find out Booker is back again, and to see his hands, oh God, his hands . . ."

Con drew her to his solid chest, her lithe tiny frame so strong, yet topped by such a fragile psyche.

"Honey girl, listen . . . listen to me. It's all a game with Booker. The world's all astir, a senator kidnapped, all the glare of mobilized urgency and bustle. But this is the real, serious part of the game. Penelope, he *wants* me to find him. These pictures are traceable; something in them will help us find them. But he wants me crazy first. He wants me crazy to find him and kill him. He wants me to think about his hands on Maggie. Okay, I'm thinking. But until I reach her, she's safe. She knows that, too. She'll endure this.

"But it's this team—and me in particular—that he wants. He wants us to blunder our way to him and get ourselves slaughtered in the process. He's prodding the public, pushing

45

the politics of it, the captured senator, national security and all that crap. But all he wants is us, and we have to find a way to get him, and get Maggie and her dad out. We have to use our heads in this and keep our hearts out. Do you understand? We have to be steady and sure, so that this time he stays dead."

Penelope didn't say anything for a while, then she stepped back and put the pictures back in their bright blue I.D. envelope with the 21A stamp on it. "Picture interpretation, right?" she said with arched brows.

"Yeah. Tell them I need whatever they can dig up, preferably where they were taken. I doubt they can get that, but they might find something."

"I'll take care of it, Con. Don't worry about me. I'm bloody all right. We Brits have starch."

Thirty minutes later, an F-5 courier fighter jet took off for the CIA photo interpretation and intelligence lab at Langley, Virginia.

The photos of Booker's assault on Maggie during the staged photo session were different in more than one way from the placid set sent to the White House for press exposure. Maggie had unthinkingly reacted to his sexual assault and in pulling away, she had spread the field of focus wider than Booker had thought.

Two things showed in one set that did not show in the other. The roof of one of the smaller villas was partially visible, and after intensification, the pattern of the odd, Mexican-like red tile was clearly visible. Also in the picture, a thin sliver of unfurled sail jutted into the blue background. Computer enhancement brought out numbers printed on its opposite side. AK6: three of what would be a seven- or eight-digit registration number. Not much, but more than they'd hoped for.

Predator Bay
7:00 A.M. January 2, 1994

Maggie awoke as if shot from a cannon. Caribbean breezes

filtered through her bedroom, the lacy curtains, so out of place here, blowing in and out the open window. She caught myriad scents on the air: tropical flowers, sea and salt, heat, and strongest of all, coffee. Her room was dappled in shadow and light, the sun low but already warm. The surf, even three hundred yards away, lapped at the beach with a steady, sodden slapping sound. In any other situation, at any other time, this spot might have seemed like paradise on Earth.

There was a quick rap at her door, and one of her impassive guards, a dark-skinned man without identifiable nationality, walked into the room with a breakfast tray, set it down across her knees, and left the room. Karen Black, carrying a bloody Mary and wearing the tiniest thong bikini without the top, trailed in as he left and sat down delicately in a rattan chair near the bed. Her breasts were heavy and full with small pink nipples. Someday, if she lived that long, thought Maggie, Karen Black, soft and round now, would be fat and droopy. Or at least Maggie hoped so.

"What have you got against modesty?" Maggie asked in a listless tone.

"Nothin'! Just like to be . . . available is the word. I brought your father his breakfast and he was glad to see me."

"I'll just bet he was. Coffee and big tits for breakfast. An old Virginia standby."

"Don't forget blow jobs. He had one of those, too." She shifted in her chair, an obscene little wiggle. Maggie started to protest, saw the look of female triumph in Karen's eyes, and knew the woman was telling the truth. She tried to keep her mind level, on keel. This was a wicked place, and wicked games were played here. She'd have to harden her heart and toughen her mind.

"I hope he enjoyed it," she said, acting even more bored than before.

"Oh, I can guarantee that. For a moment there, when I took him all the way down my throat, I thought he might be having an attack of some kind. He said that had never happened to him before. I told him it might bloody well never happen again, either. He's down at the beach now, like a whale thrown up from the sea, catching the rays of our tropical paradise. That's right out of a travel brochure I saw once in the middle of winter in London. I was freezing my clit off then, and now look where I am."

Maggie sipped her coffee, uncomfortable but growing accustomed to Karen's nakedness. The girl had no morals and no mind whatsoever.

"What does he do for you, Karen, to enslave you like this?"

"Who?"

"Booker."

"Oh, you mean Mr. Brooks. Nothing. It's what I do for him that counts. This morning he told me to suck your father's dick. So, I sucked a dick. There are nice times with Mr. Brooks. He's quite good in bed—a bit peculiar and very rough—but I'm adjusting to it. And he gives me the loveliest little hypo twice a day. I don't know what it is, but I like it. He bought me a sailboat. That little one, the thirty-footer. Someday, he says, he'll find me a sailor to go with it." Karen looked at Maggie with wide, glowing eyes, eyes unnaturally bright and excited. Drugs, and powerful ones at that.

"How long have you been with Mr. Book—er, Mr. Brooks?"

"Oh, a long time. I met him on Christmas Eve one year."

"What year, Karen?"

"Just last. Only a week or so ago, actually. It takes very little time to get to be Mr. Brooks's friend. He told me enemies take longer to develop and need more cultivating. He told me your old man is his best enemy, whatever that means."

"My father?"

"No, your lover, Mr. Duggan, I think. He intends to kill your lover. Right here on this island. Did you know that?"

"Yes, Karen, I know that."

"Good. Put on a suit or something, and come down to the beach. Might as well enjoy it while you can."

For the life of her, Maggie couldn't think of a single reason not to do just that.

The photos and those who studied them were driving two different rescue groups along the same road, but with different results. General Cassidy took one obvious option: To him, wherever his senator was, it was tropical and would, therefore, require those elements of Delta Force that trained most often in for that environment. He initially selected an elite parachute team that could be dropped, it was said, right in your living room. He excused all other Delta Force units, settling on a Navy SEAL assault unit to augment the paratroopers. This unit was comprised of twenty-eight SEALS who were experts in attacking from the sea. He was feeling mean and lean, making decisions, yet he still had no hard evidence as to where the senator was.

Paxton, New Mexico
1:35 P.M. January 2, 1994

The man saw the Ford Bronco long before it reached his trailer, a plume of yellowish dust streaming behind it as it raced along the dirt road toward him. Two hundred yards away, his business partners put down their chemicals and gathered outside the second trailer on the desolate lot.

A coyote jumped out of the Bronco's path and trotted off, tail up, pissed off and rabbitless. The Bronco had done it a favor by running over its dinner.

The four men watched, but didn't move. One of the three men at the second trailer, a massive, bearded, tattooed, virgin's nightmare, held a sawed-off pump 12-gauge shotgun in one meaty hand.

The Bronco, painted black and with heavily tinted windows, roared to a stop, throwing dirt behind it in waves. Two miles back, along the dirt road, the dust was settling again, erasing the truck's passage. The Bronco sat there, its small driver nearly invisible in the cab. Finally, the door swung open, and a petite young woman wearing cowboy boots, denim shorts, and a tight white T-shirt jumped out.

"Jesus Christ", she muttered, "only mad dogs and Englishmen! Which one of you blokes is Gregory Wolf?" Penelope James was alone and looked very sexy indeed. As soon as she hit the ground, the one-hundred degree heat started her sweating. She wore a Browning 9mm pistol on one slim hip.

"Who wants to know, honey?" The hairy beast with the tattoos and the shotgun was the questioner. He had stepped forward from the second trailer.

"I do. Penelope James, late of the United Kingdom and presently an illegal alien in your country. Are you Mr. Wolf?"

"Now that all depends."

"Does it now! On what?"

"On how important it is for you to talk to this Mr. Wolf guy."

"It's very. I'm prepared to pay."

"I'll bet you are, honey." There was a leer on his face that was echoed in his voice.

"Don't even think of it, you bloody cretin." Penelope was genuinely offended at the tacit suggestion.

"Spunk. I like that in a gal." He began to walk toward her in a kind of rolling shuffle, the biker walk. The three were members of the Desert Angels Motorcycle Club, an outlaw spin-off more dangerous than the original Hell's Angels band. The second trailer was a ten-million-dollar-a-year drug lab that produced speed and various hallucinogens.

"Do you know what 'spunk' means in Britain?"

The man kept walking toward her, the same leering smile on his face. "Nope. What's it mean, honey?"

"It means semen. Cum. You know, that stuff that comes out of your prick when you wank off." Penelope's hand moved swiftly to her waist, and when it came back up, it held a 9mm handgun loaded with explosive rounds. "I could shoot your little wanker right off, if you'd like."

The man froze. Penelope fixed the man's gaze with her own and said, "Now be a gentleman, and tell me where I might find Mr. Wolf. I'm pressed for time. My plane leaves

that convenient little airstrip of yours in one hour. I must be
on it."

"Your plane?"

"Of course. How else did you think I got here?"

"Well, honey, you picked the wrong day to visit. Wrong
place, too. No Mr. Wolf here."

"I said I have little time, and I'll pay for the information
I need. I want to know about a type of red tile I'm told can
only be made by Mr. Wolf. If I'm incorrect about that, I'll
still pay for the information."

"You ain't listenin', honey. And you ain't gonna make
your train, neither."

"I have no bloody time for this!" The 9mm roared out,
shattering the desert stillness, the shotgun stock, and the
man's knee, all in sequence.

"Jesus! You shot me!" The man rolled slowly over on
the ground, one knee bent awkwardly and torn open.

"So I did. And I shall shoot you again if necessary."

The gun waved like a snake, its ugly snout settling on
the man's forehead. The other two men stayed near the
trailer. The silent man outside the other trailer, standing
amid a cluster of sculptures in progress, finally spoke. "I'm
Gregory Wolf. Put that thing down. You two, put the stupid
ass on the flatbed. Get him fixed up before he bleeds to
death. Take him over to Doc Carrigan. Hell, a horse doc
is all that drunken old man needs."

"Why didn't you speak up?"

"Strange world, strange people. Strange times. Hell, old
Buck spoke up, and you shot him. What do you do to people
you *really* don't like?" He gave her a smile, although she
was unable to read its sincerity since he wore mirrored
sunglasses.

"Your work, all this?"

"Hobby. It's work when you make a living off it. I get
five thousand dollars in rent from my chemistry friends. It
tides me over, buys cat food. Why don't we get over the
chitchat? What do you want?"

"Very well. Let's do that. You do architectural work,
don't you?"

"Not anymore. Nobody gives a shit about quality or artistic decoration. It's not the money. Plenty of that around. Nobody cares anymore."

He turned away, and resumed work on a torso of a woman. Just arms and breasts. Penelope walked to his side and studied his work.

"You have nice hands. Nice work. But she has no head, no face."

"True. I don't like women enough to give her a face. Women are bad for you."

"Are you celibate then?" Her bantering tone, her usual sexy way of arousing men, stopped his work. He took off his glasses; his eyes were very clear, very blue, very intense.

"No, I fuck women. I just don't put their faces on my work. Your face is interesting. Perhaps you could change my mind." It was both a statement and a question.

"That might be a nice thing to explore one day, but not now. Perhaps another time."

"A raincheck?"

"Oh, yes. That's American for looking into or doing something later, isn't it?"

"Yeah, sort of."

"Fine. A raincheck it is. Perhaps I'll just fly in some night when you need a face for your work."

"Do you always shoot people?"

"No, not always."

"Than I'll look forward to it."

"Look at these photographs, please, Mr. Wolf."

"Gregory."

"Oh yes, we have a raincheck, don't we? First name appropriate. Please, I have little time. And I have ten thousand dollars cash in the Bronco if you can tell me anything about this photo."

"My, my. Ten Gs."

"Quite."

The artist wiped his hands on a work apron and studied the photos. He handed them back to Penelope.

"Did you design them, Gregory?"

"How did you come to that conclusion?"

"I didn't, SCAR did."

"SCAR?"

"Security Caretaker and Research. It's a computer, a very special one. It took it almost three minutes to match the art with the artist. It took forty more seconds to track you from place to place to here."

"How?"

"Don't know, exactly, but the last piece of information it gave us was the trailer registration number and location. So here I am. Now can you tell me anything?"

"Listen, lady, this is all a bit weird for me, even when you consider my lifestyle. Who is 'us'? Who are you?"

"It doesn't matter. I'll tell you this. It means a woman's life and the life of a United States Senator."

"Oh, yeah. I heard about that. But I don't know anything of any value. I don't know where they are, which seems to be your main problem. Hell, they're kidnapped! The bad guys'll tell you where to find them."

"We want to find them first, Gregory. Your government will be grateful for whatever help you provide."

"You mean you won't shut my business down and bust me?"

"Yes, that's what I mean."

"Fine. Now all the bullshit is over. The ten grand was a cheap woman's trick, though. The threats are plenty."

Penelope turned around and walked to the Bronco, her lithe body sending its usual messages as she moved. She opened the door, reached in, and pulled a small leather exercise bag out, and tossed it to him.

"As I said, ten thousand—in fresh tens and twenties. Now tell me what you can. With SCAR, anything might help."

Gregory Wolf looked at the photographs again, carefully this time, the bag full of fresh new money hanging off his wrist.

"I used to do a lot of stuff like this: floor and wall tiles, bathrooms, walkways. Not very many people could afford to do a roof. I did a couple."

"Did you do this one, Gregory?"

"And if I did?"

"Who for, Gregory?"

"Well, this guy's not going to be of any help to you. Word's out, oh, must be over a year now. Bad gun deal. Somebody blew him up. He's dead."

"Even so, the house didn't go with him. Who was this man?"

"Booker was his name. Baddest dude I ever met. Crazy, I think. I did some work on his yacht, very delicate stuff. Belongs in a museum, not on a boat. Blown all to hell, I hear."

"I'm sorry, Gregory, about your art being blown up, but where do you think this house is?"

"I didn't install it, I just designed and made it. Forged each one myself, right here. He flew in every once in a while, up until his boat took him to sailor heaven. For a few years in the late eighties, I was doing a dozen or more commissions for him each year. He was a very bad man. I knew him off and on way back, starting with Viet Nam, I guess. I probably have a couple of these tiles in my shed somewhere. I like to keep examples of my work. The formula for the adhesive and color-lock in these is my secret. A hundred years in the sun, and they still won't fade."

"All this is wonderful, and I appreciate it. May I have a tile to take with me?"

"Sure, you paid ten grand for it."

She walked with him to a long falling-down shed. The inside was a sharp contrast to the dilapidated exterior. The floor was clean and waxed, and the space was well lighted and crammed with busts, statues, bowls, and other examples of the man's work over the past twenty or so years.

"Some shed," Penelope said wryly, her eyes wide.

"Yeah, well, this is the serious stuff, I guess. Here, on the back wall, in that wooden case, that's Booker's tile. Take it if you want it."

Penelope swung over to the wall and plucked it out of its holder. "Why, the design is made up entirely of little letters of the alphabet!" she said after examining it for a moment.

"Yeah, he was a weird guy. Each tile was different. Thousands and thousands of *Peter Coy Booker*s over and over again, mixed up, sideways, up and down. I did twenty thousand of them by hand. He paid me a hundred thousand dollars."

"My God!"

"Yeah, like I said, he was weird."

"One more question, Gregory. Do you remember when and where you shipped those twenty thousand thousand-dollar-per-copy tiles?"

"As a matter of fact, I do."

Penelope's heart jumped, thudding loud enough for her to feel it. "When?"

"December, 1979."

"Where?"

"Miami, Florida. Where they went from there, I don't know. I never saw them installed. I never saw the house, but I think it's on an island."

"Why?"

"Hell, the man goes everywhere by boat. Most everywhere in the world he lived had boating access and maintenance facilities. I did a couple of brass lions for a place he had on the Mediterranean. Some unnamed Greek island, just his house and a few others clinging to a cliff over the dock. The guy told me once he had twenty homes around the world. He moved a lot, practically every month. He was a very security-conscious guy."

"So, you think the house is near Miami."

"No, I don't, but that's where I shipped the tiles. He told me it was for an island place. The tile color compliments the orchids he grows there, but I have no idea what island that might be."

"Gregory, you've been more than helpful."

"Yeah, well, why not? Ten thousand and a pretty girl in the bargain."

"I'm not in the bargain, Gregory."

"Yeah, well, ya never know. Besides, Peter Coy Booker is dead. Believe me, if he was alive, I wouldn't've told you anything."

"Don't worry, Gregory. When I see him, I won't mention your name. Goodbye." She stood on her tiptoes and gave him a soft peck on the lips, then raced to the truck, tile in hand, and roared back down the dirt road. The rabbit had long since been picked up by the angry coyote.

Back at the shed, Gregory Wolf watched the car until it disappeared under its long cloud of dust. Out loud, to no one in particular, he voiced a sudden disquieting thought, "What the fuck did she mean, 'When I see him, I won't mention your name.'?"

7

Chin sat on a marble bench, sweat-soaked after his long workout with Booker. He wiped his shaved head with a bright towel decorated with Booker's favorite image, the jungle tiger. There were representations of tigers everywhere on the walls throughout the compound.

Chin draped the towel around his neck and strolled to the open lanai, sprawling into a deck chair, trying to catch a sea breeze. Soft breezes, a tropical paradise, a fantasy. And truly, it was, as he watched Karen Black and the captive, Maggie Stuart, spread out on the beach like basting animals, sleek with oil and languid from the heat.

He shifted his view away from the peaceful scene, but not before he noticed Karen Black stand up and walk to the "extra" captive, the out-of-shape, sorrowful Senator Stuart. Karen Black began to apply oil to his body, and in seconds was straddling him. What kind of man would allow a woman to seduce him less than fifty yards from his daughter? A weak man, a vain man, a man who was frightened, yet arrogant, and somehow not able to hide either emotion.

Chin turned to watch Booker, his lifetime employer, as he whipped his body around the wooden-walled dojo, working to become proficient in the martial arts with only one real hand. Booker had determined that the leather hand and its claw-like set of warped fingers was in and of itself a weapon.

57

Mastering that weapon, however, was proving difficult.

Superbly trained experts, even those at Chin's exalted level, had always had trouble competing with Booker. Now, as a result of his long hospitalization, Booker was in the least competitive shape of his life. The deformed hand had to be compensated for; it altered his balance. In their workouts together, Chin had been able to attack the deficient left side of Booker's body repeatedly. But Peter Coy Booker was a fanatic in all things. He lengthened his workout time and had mastered many mechanical weapons, from pistols to machine guns. Still, Chin felt Booker would never again reach his former prowess in the martial arts. Martin Brooks would never have been able to beat Peter Coy Booker.

Soon Chin's long-time associate joined him on the lanai, an identical towel around his neck. Booker's body had rehardened itself with all this work, but he was still lighter by twenty pounds. Even so, his new appearance was arresting, to say the least. His skin, no matter how much sun he got, remained pink and alabaster smooth. His altered bone structure and nearly white hair, combined with eyes that seemed at times insane and at other times dead, made him a devastatingly handsome man. Pretty, almost. Women, Chin had noticed, often stopped in their tracks, right on the street, to look at him. Karen Black, in her trampy way, thought he was the most handsome man she had ever seen, and she had reminded them that she had seen quite a few in her twenty-three years.

"Look at them—the senator is having quite a time," Booker observed with a sardonic smile.

"Yes sir, but he dishonors his daughter."

"Oh shit, Chin, don't go all bloody Eastern on me. He's like all men around an available cunt. He'll fuck her because she'll fuck him."

"His daughter lies quietly on the same beach," Chin persisted.

"Oh, Maggie Stuart's a tough girl, plenty tough. She spent eighteen years with Con Duggan. Before we kill her, I'm going to find out why."

"It is unimportant, sir. She is bait, very good bait. Killing her is of no value to us."

"Oh. Since when did killing upset you?"

"Business is business. Sometimes killing is part of business."

"Well, look at this as business."

"Not necessary. Killing Mr. Duggan is a matter of personal honor and is to be admired. Killing the woman is a snake hunting a mongoose in its own lair and not advisable."

"She's part of it."

"No. Even the lamb tied to the stake for the leopard by the hunter is released after the leopard is killed. It is a lamb. It is bait, no more. You were blinded by her availability. You moved a year sooner than you had planned, simply because she was briefly available. Now we have collected a lion with the lamb, and we are being hunted."

"That's the bloody idea, isn't it?"

"Yes, but it will not be Con Duggan who hunts us. It will be handed over to the politicians, because we have one of the brotherhood. *Her* name would never have appeared in the papers. Now the entire government will be after us."

"True, but Con Duggan will find us, because we *want* him to find us."

"We moved too fast."

Booker leaned toward Chin, his blue eyes alight with something from beyond the dead. "Don't you remember, Chin? That bus shooting us to pieces, blowing us out of the water, taking my hand?" The leather hand grabbed Chin's thigh, painfully, and seemingly of its own will. "Remember the *Stingray,* all my artwork, who I was? *I* remember. A wall of fire racing across the water and sweeping over my face. *You* saw, you remember. I've waited, and now I've waited long enough!" The grip on Chin's thigh loosened, and the deranged look went out of Booker's eyes. "C'mon, friend, let's go talk to the senator."

Champ Stuart held his breath as Karen Black squatted over his thighs and gripped him with her eager young hand, guiding him into her. He felt his cock slide into her heat, her muscles gripping him, sucking him up into her.

"Oh, you like that, don't you, Senator?" Her hips began to rotate in tight little circles as he grasped at her breasts, sleek and slippery with tanning oil. He started to come, but she reached back and gripped the base of his cock and squeezed. "Oh no, not yet, Senator. Baby, Mama's not bloody ready yet. Keep your spunk till I tell you, or I'll just stop." She settled down on him, her fingers flicking her clit and nipples, her breath getting ragged.

"Don't stop, Karen, please."

"Please! Oh, that's a nice word. Let it soak a bit, love. I'll move real slow now. Riding this old pot belly of yours is fun, Senator, but you need to get in better shape, don't you think?" She leaned forward, forcing a breast into his mouth. He suckled at her like a baby, his skinny legs covered with sand stuck to his oiled body. She resumed her little circles and added short, sharp bumps, cooing in his ear. "Do you love Mommie's tits? Tell me you love Mommie's tits."

"I love your tits, Mommie. Please, don't stop."

He opened his eyes as a shadow crossed his face and saw, upside down, the smiling countenance of Martin Brooks and the somber face of Chin.

"Senator! How are you making out? Don't get up on our account. We'll talk like we are. Please, don't stop your activities. We like our kidnap victims to experience the very best the tropics have to offer."

Karen Black sat up and leaned back, startled by her employer's appearance. Well, he'd instructed her to do this as often as the old man could get it up!

"Keep the service going, you beautiful girl. The senator and I will just talk while you play."

Champ Stuart tried to get up, and Karen pinned him down, her arms moving to his chest, her vaginal muscles clamping onto him. In spite of shame, embarrassment, and fear, he didn't go soft, and he didn't try to move again.

"There, I knew you could do it. You're a very virile man, Senator. Karen is talented, don't you think? Some of the things she does. . . . Oh, my. . . ."

Champ Stuart couldn't believe what was happening to him, and he suddenly started to go soft inside her. She reached behind and grabbed him, shifted him, moving him, and then he was caught, tighter than before, more exotic than before, and he couldn't pull away.

"Tell me, Senator, who do you think will attempt to rescue you?"

"I, I don—" His breathing was jagged.

"Of course, you don't know who will come, but who do you think might visit us?"

"Let me . . . let me . . . I think . . ."

"Finish him, Karen. Clearly, the senator can't think and fuck at the same time."

She threw herself forward, shifted, and began to move rapidly. "Go on, darlin'. Come now. Come in Mommie's ass. Yes, that's where you are, in Mommie's . . ."

With that, he erupted inside her while two men, his kidnappers, watched. He strained up at her, and she threw her head back, her breath coming in short little barking cries, her fingers busy at her vagina until she climaxed and rolled off him. She let out a long sigh just as her breathing returned to normal.

"Well, you talk now, gentlemen. I'm going for a swim. See you soon, Senator. Don't worry, Mommie'll keep it warm for you."

Naked, soaked with her, sand in every crevice of his body, he kept his eyes averted and sat up.

"Good, Senator. You're *very* good. Why don't you go shower? We'll talk later."

They watched as the influential senator, a man of enormous power and prestige, walked wordlessly away, skinny-legged, pot-bellied, covered with sand. And shame.

"Did you enjoy that, sir?" Chin inquired with a trace of disdain in his voice.

"What's enjoyment got to do with it, Chin? It's all about control, now isn't it? He's a U.S. Senator—I'm a criminal. We're just establishing the rules here at Predator Bay. Here, I'm in charge."

"There are limits."

"Well, we'll see what they are, then. Let's go visit the fair Maggie Stuart. Perhaps she'll critique her father's performance."

The two men headed toward the reclining form of the person Chin referred to as "tiger's bait." But Maggie, unlike her father, would prove to be more tiger than bait.

Maggie was aware of the two men's presence but kept her eyes closed, not acknowledging them.

"Can we talk, Miss Stuart?" Booker's voice was soft but without warmth.

"Would you go away if I said no?"

"Is that a serious question?"

"No, it isn't." She sat up and then stood up, brushing the sand from her body with a beach towel. She was dressed in a fairly modest bikini, deliberately chosen to show Booker she didn't fear him. Her reasoning was simple. If he wanted her naked, she was helpless to stop him, and sunbathing required relatively bare skin. She was showing him she didn't care whether he looked at her body or not.

"You look very fetching." Brooker's tone was matter-of-fact, not appreciative.

"Do I? Sorry."

"Did you know who I was at the hotel ballroom?"

"Obviously not, or I wouldn't be here."

"Are you afraid?"

"Not for myself, no."

"Ah, Con. Even separated, you fear for him."

"No, I meant my father. Con can take care of himself."

"How true! Who knows more about that than I? In all these years, whenever our paths have crossed at sporting events or shooting matches, you've always been unfailingly polite, even nice, to me. Why was that? You certainly didn't like me."

"It takes very little to be polite. Con hated you, but somehow relished competing against you. Your face has changed. Nice job, I suppose, if you like that kind of thing."

"You wouldn't have liked the way I looked after the . . . ah . . . accident. Fire does terrible things. Con Duggan owes me two million dollars in medical expenses. But I'll settle for killing him."

"He won't come here. The White House won't let him. The Delta Force will be here. That's Papa's pet project in the military."

"Your father is an interesting man."

"I'm glad he's provided you with some amusement."

"Did that distress you, what you saw?"

"I didn't watch. You don't have to look at something like that. You did, though. Do you like to watch, Booker? Is that how you get yours—putting an old man through something like that? He'll never forget it."

"He's done worse, I suspect. He didn't struggle much."

"He's . . . he's not himself. Once . . . once, long ago, he'd have fucked her and beat you to death at the same time."

"Once, perhaps. Not now."

"No, not now. That was the cruelest thing I've ever seen."

"Oh, you *did* watch. Well, Con will save you."

"No, he won't."

"Oh, but I'll give him reason to save you."

"I'm not afraid."

"Yes, I can see that now, but everyone's afraid at one time or another. We'll talk later."

As the two men turned to walk away, Maggie halted them with her voice. "If Con Duggan comes here, he'll kill you. Whatever you do to my father or me won't matter. When he comes—if he comes—he'll finish the job the fire didn't do. You're dead, Booker. You just don't know it yet."

Booker looked back at her, started to say something, and checked himself. Perhaps you're right, he thought. We shall see, won't we?

He left her there, alone and cold in the warm sunshine.

8

The SCAR computer had hunted down over one hundred custom sailmakers across the nation. The trail of the roof tiles led to Miami, so the computer broke down the list yet again, first into the sailmakers on the east coast, narrower still to the southeast, and finally, Miami and South Florida. The thinking was that if the tiles went to Miami, the chances were good the boat and its sails originated there as well. The sails in the photo revealed, after computer enhancement, a quarter-inch band of red, identified after further query to SCAR as a special elasticized thread new to the sailmaking trade. It functioned as an additional bond incorporated during the end-sew process and made the sail both more durable and distinct. It was a new and very expensive process.

SCAR narrowed the list once more, which is how Steven Dye, overdressed for the hot southern Florida heat in leather pants and jacket, found himself at the broken-down entrance to a shop named Omar The Tent Maker. Tents, not sails. SCAR, however, identified the shop as a likely source of flexible thread sales. So Steven would see Omar the Tent Maker about sails.

A set of brass bells tinkled over his head, set loose by the severe bang administered by a front door that stuck and required a hard push to open. Steven Dye found himself in a large airless room, cluttered from end to end with canvas in various stages of manufacture. Across the room, stairs led in a spiral sweep upward into what he thought might be a sailmaker's loft. This was the first place on SCAR's list of possibilities, and Steven was hoping for a bit of Penelope's luck. Her first call had been a strike.

The room seemed empty, and then a large igloo-shaped tent in the middle of the floor began to move and rumble. From it emerged a gray-bearded man of enormous girth, three hundred pounds or so, and standing six-feet-six or more.

For a big man, he had a surprisingly quiet, small voice. "We're closed," he said, his lips nearly invisible in the beard.

"Sorry. Your door was open."

"Nope. It was closed. That's as closed as it gets, having to push it open like that. 'Course, you couldn't of known that. Sarah, come on out here, gal. Never mind your hair an' such."

A woman as small and slim as the bearded man was big and fat popped out of the same igloo-shaped tent, trying frantically to pull her panties on.

"Damn! Backwards and inside out!" She pulled them off, turned them right side out, shook them once, and put first her left foot, then her right into them. Then she bent over and pulled them up her legs and over her buttocks. All without a trace of self-consciousness or modesty.

"We *do* close here, mister," the woman said. " 'Bout four P.M. most days. Andy and me, we get sort of horny about that time, and if we get horny, he fucks me. He don't pay me much, so he fucks me instead. But since you're here, we'll sell you a tent, if you'd like."

"You sell a lot of tents here?"

"Sure! And why not? Damn Everglades is practically outside the door. Camping is big business, don't you know that?"

"Well, I certainly do now, but I actually came to talk to you about custom sails."

"We don't do sails anymore. More money in tents. Right, Andy?"

Andy, finally properly zipped and together, nodded. "I prefer sails, but we can't support eight kids on what I make on sails."

"Eight?"

"Yup. Married this little lady when she was twelve. Thirty, now, but still good enough for me. I love sailmakin', but yuppies come in here, see these hand-sewn tents I do, and plop down twelve hundred bucks or so like it was nothin'. Tents pay the bills, so I quit makin' sails."

"Were you good at it?"

"You know anything about sailin', boy?"

"Not much. I've sailed, but just Chesapeake Bay stuff. Fourteen-, sixteen-footers. No multi-sails or any sea time. Kid stuff."

"Well, I don't make kid stuff. Racing sails, mostly twelve meter and up, but it takes too much time, and I won't sell my stuff cheap. Tents ain't much—but sails—sails are *something!*"

"When did you last make sails?"

"Oh, a year or two back, maybe three. Why's that important?"

"Because I'm looking for one particular set of sails. These sails incorporate special threading techniques, the best Kelvar blends, a quarter-inch red counterstitch of some kind. They're multifold, with back-cross hand stitching, and special dyes were used for both ropes and sails. Needless to say, these sails were very, very expensive."

"And you think I make those special sails?"

"Well, did you?"

"I might have. It all depends on what I might recall with . . . ah . . . with the proper prodding of my memory. Memory's a fine thing, worth a lot, 'specially if it's fadin' fast."

"*If* you get his meaning," the woman added. She had very large breasts and had carelessly let her blouse fall open to prove it.

"I think I get his meaning. How much do you think it might take to start him remembering if he made the sails I need?"

"To start? Well, about a hundred."

Steven Dye pulled a wad of bills from his pocket and peeled five hundreds from it. He walked to the big tent, crawled over piles of tent and awning material, and handed the bills to the slight woman. She glanced at them and put them in her dress pocket. "That starts it up pretty good, sonny. 'Course, it may run down a time or two. Memory's often in need of financial prodding."

"Fine. Let's start with simple stuff. Did you make this sail?"

Andy studied the photo set for a moment and muttered, "Think I did, yeah. Think so."

"For who?"

"Now *who* I made it for—I might be less inclined to tell you that. I did make the sail. Four sets, identical—I can get you the ID numbers. Those are hand sewn. This little gal did that. Pregnant at the time, if I recall."

"Sure was," she said. "With Esther. Big as a house and trying to haul two hundred six square feet of sail around the loft. And that 'Red Power' thread! Great stuff, but hard to find. Material's from Cambodia, of all places. Our client had over a thousand square yards of trim, and he provided all the Red Power."

"Yup. Then he charged *us* for it. Hard man."

"You won't tell me his name?"

"*Can't* tell you."

"Why?"

"Never met him, that's why. This big Oriental guy did the deal and picked up the sails. Chin, I think he said his name was. But I never saw the buyer." Andy placed his huge hand on the woman's breast, and pulled savagely on her nipple. She seemed to enjoy it immensely, and it didn't distract her from the subject at hand.

"We know the guy's name," she admitted, "but he has bad friends. So we don't know it, understand?"

"Was his name Booker?"

The couple stiffened but gave no other sign that Booker was their client. "No name. Sorry." Andy said it, but they shook their heads.

"Well, I know Booker, so I understand your fear. How about the boat?" Steven hoped that taking a different tack might yield better results.

"The name? Don't know."

Steven Dye peeled off a thousand dollars and counted it slowly, so they could add it up. Then he said, "Okay, but surely you knew what kind of boat you were making sails for."

"Oh, sure . . . can't recall it, tho'."

"Sorry to bother you then." Steven put the cash back on the roll and put it in his pocket.

The woman would have none of that. "Two thousand, and I'll look and see if it's in our files. We kept 'em on boats. We don't bother on tents."

"Check the files, then. If you have anything of value, the two thousand is yours, and I'm gone."

She turned away and went up the spiral staircase, stopping just short of the loft area. She turned around, and as she stood there ten feet above them, Steven could look straight up her dress. She unbuttoned it and held it open. Her figure was almost *too* lush, but only almost.

"Omar likes to watch other men fuck me. You interested?"

"Sorry, perhaps another time."

"No problem. Remember me, though."

"You got the hard body this little ole gal loves," Andy said with a genuine smile. "Like you said, perhaps another time."

She buttoned up her dress and disappeared up the last stair and onto the sail level.

"Interesting woman, that one." Steven could think of nothing more clever to say.

"Ain't she, though. Got a half-inch clit. Like a little dick."

"I'll keep that in mind."

"You boys come up here," she called down to them. "I found something on that damn boat." In spite of his bulk, Omar was up the circular stairway before Steven could react. It was like following a huge pair of overalls stuffed with barbells.

The loft had all the discipline the tent area did not. The walls were covered with the tools of the sailmaker's trade, neatly ready to swing into action if required. It was spotlessly clean, the floor waxed to a high polish, the wood old and pitted with the occasional roll or bend advertising its age. Omar and his wife lost a great deal of their "hick" personas in this space.

"Here we are. The main sail was 1200 feet square, eight hundred sixty square feet for the foretriangle. It was a customized variation of a Bënêteau Oceanis 350, displacement 11,000 pounds, 34 feet, 10 inches long. It had an auxiliary 29-horsepower Volvo 2003. Briand/Cushing design, standard design by Briand of a boat introduced first in 1986, and Cushing made a few, delicate changes. Sleeps 8. Head is extra large, black marble. It's heavy, and that costs it two knots in speed. Our special sails compensated for the loss and added speed, and the ultramodern reef sail system makes it easy to handle. That replaced the original Goiot roller furling system. The boat was painted with twelve individual coats of Packard Royal Deep Purple. The boat is very beautiful, I suppose, but we were never allowed to see it. The boat was rebuilt in Charlotte, North Carolina, by Bënêteau (USA) Ltd. Sails and boat joined and both active in 1991. That's all I have. Here's a picture of her, full sail." The picture showed the boat leaning into a wave, crystal-white wake and spray highlighting its beautiful paint job.

"It's pretty, all right. Fast, too?"

"Fairly. It's not a racer exactly, but it can blow away your average, high-weight, big-cash sailboat."

"Just like Booker."

"I beg your pardon?" Culture seemed to come with the loft, and simply by entering it, she had acquired a considerable amount.

"Booker . . . your client. Nothing about him is ever what it seems. For instance, he has an annoying habit of returning from the dead."

This time, all pretense disappeared. Genuine fear flashed broadly across the sailmakers' faces. A chill passed over the room.

"May I keep the photo?" Steven asked.

"Sure, you paid two thousand dollars for it."

Reminded, Steven Dye pulled the roll from his pocket and flipped it toward the couple. This time Andy intercepted it in flight, right in front of his wife's extended hands.

"Nice catch. There's a little over three thousand there. Consider the rest a tip."

"Don't forget our offer, Mr. . . ."

"Dye, Steven Dye."

"And don't forget, the offer was serious. Sailing, sex, and sex and sailing, that's what we do." She gave Steven a mischievous smile.

"That and your tents."

"Yes, those too."

"Do you really have eight kids?"

"No, my tubes were tied years ago."

"I'll remember your offer. By the way, is there anything you'd like me to tell Mr. Booker if I see him?" That comment left Andy and his wife speechless.

Steven pocketed the photo of the sailboat and headed down the spiral staircase. The couple came together at the top, and he got one last look up her dress. Then he used their phone to make transportation arrangements and headed for North Carolina. He had the sailmaker, and he knew where the boat was built. Match the two, and perhaps he could find the boat itself, maybe even the island where it was moored. In his first solo effort for the Confirmed Kill Team, he'd been as lucky as Penelope.

Soon, he knew, the luck would stop, but he hoped that wouldn't happen until they matched the puzzle pieces and hung them around Peter Coy Booker's homicidal neck.

Predator Bay
1:00 A.M. January 3, 1994

Peter Coy Booker sat on the teak deck of the object of Steven Dye's frantic search looking shoreward. His house, all white except for its spectacular red roof, seemed to glow and shimmer in the moonlight, its arches and ovals and stark rectangular entrances a mishmash that somehow coalesced into seamless, fitting beauty. Only Lord Glenconner's Taj Mahal-esque Great House on the island of Mustique compared. Glenconner's home was one of many famous residences throughout the Caribbean owned by wealthy princesses, princes, politicians, and rock stars. Here on Predator Bay, far off the tourist beat, Booker's exquisite island house stood unknown and precious as a rare pearl still harbored inside an oyster at the bottom of the sea. It had cost four million to build, including power generators, an airfield, and twenty smaller buildings for his staff of thugs, murderers, and gangsters.

Predator Bay. Booker hadn't used the island since 1991. He'd brought the *Stingray* here once and stayed to meet a Kurdish gun runner. The deal hadn't worked out, and the Kurdish party wound up as fish food.

He could see the single reading light in the bedroom of the villa near his house and watch her movements as she alternately read and paced back and forth across the room. Separated by only two hundred yards of beach and an eighty-foot dock, he could see her clearly through the gauzy curtains that draped the retractable sixteen-foot window facing the sea. He centered the twenty-power telescope on her face and looked at it, a voyeur kidnapper who had his prize and now wanted to play with it. He picked up the deck phone.

"Sir?" the voice at the distant end asked.

"Bring her to me."

"Now, sir?"

"Yes, idiot!"

"Of course, sir." The wire went silent, and he watched the shadowy form of one of her guards cross the open, lightly covered window, and in moments, he saw them crossing the glistening sands of the elegant beach, her silk gown flowing wakelike behind her, her black hair long and loose over her shoulders. Con Duggan's woman. Worth killing for? Dying for? Soon he'd find out.

She came aboard at the opposite end of the deck and walked toward him as he sat in the deck chair, his back to the sea, drinking Scotch and watching her legs flash in the thigh-high slit of the gown. She seemed to be completely unaware of his gaze or the look on his face, but she knew what kind of look it was. The look of a cat with a bird.

"Thank you for joining me, Miss Stuart. Please, sit here, next to me."

Maggie eyed the reclining deck chair, and then, with little fuss, sat down and didn't bother to cover her exposed legs. Perhaps, she thought, her sexuality could be used against Booker.

"Nice little boat you have here," she said to him.

"Specially built for me."

"You like things 'built' for you, don't you, Mr. Booker?"

Not a question, really, but Booker answered it anyway. "Yes, I do. Particularly people. I like people built for me. You could have been, if perfection like you possess could be found unattached. I always resented you. Con always had too many loyalties. He still does, and I believe it's you he's most loyal to. Hence, your visit here."

"Is that what I'm doing here? Visiting?"

"Perhaps not in the exact sense of the word, but you *are* my guest—until Con Duggan arrives. Then, if he survives, you may 'check out,' as it were. But he won't survive. I'll provoke him, and he'll eventually rut and stomp his way down here on his own. The Government has ordered his group to stand down, and Delta Force has the job of rescuing the senator from his—as they put it—his terrible ordeal."

"How do you know Con's been stood down?"

"Friends—I have many friends. Some are in very high places. Power, money, women: I've offered and exposed many people to those advantages. Few turn me down."

"Con Duggan turned you down," she said with a note of pride in her voice.

"He told you, did he?"

"He told me you once offered him half of your worldly goods to be your partner."

"Not half, exactly, but a goodly sum."

"No matter. He said no. He turned you down."

"Yes, and then much later, long after we'd both left the steamy regions of the Far East, he showed up in lovely

Folkestone with a murderous crew, and he tried to kill me. We're so much alike, Con Duggan and I."

"That's preposterous!"

"Is it, Maggie? Even your idyllic life in the cold nether-reaches of Alaska couldn't keep him out of the business. Your soft arms couldn't keep him home. He left you and went back to the dark hole he crawled out of. He and I recognize one thing about each other. He's capable of murder, and I'm capable of anything!"

Booker stood up, moved to Maggie's side, and struck her with a viscious blow to the face. He ripped her gown from her body, hitting her repeatedly while she tried to fight him off. She lapsed in and out of consciousness and experienced little of the rape until it was over.

Then he was gone, and she found herself alone on the deck. Maggie pulled the few remaining pieces of her nightgown off and dived naked into the warm water of Predator Bay. Her mind and her thought processes were intact. She had mentally prepared herself to be raped long before the actual event. Her body was bruised and battered, but her heart and mind were as stone. Peter Coy Booker had entered an empty vessel, and as she swam, she felt no shame, only hatred for the artificially rebuilt criminal, who she realized was totally out of his mind. Now she would have to hate him as much as he hated Con Duggan. While she swam a slow backstroke around the boat, a guard watched her, a broad, lewd smile on his face. She prayed, not for herself, but for Con. She knew they'd taken photographs, and seeing them would make him take unnecessary risks.

9

"Mr. Jackson?"

"Who wants to know? Goddamit, it's not even daylight yet!" A huge man in his underwear blocked the door.

"FBI, sir. Are you Jim Bob Jackson the Third?"

"I am, but I don't use 'the third.' Too uppity."

Steven Dye, standing behind the broad backs of two FBI agents, tried not to laugh out loud. Jim Bob had a neon flamingo in his yard, blinking on and off, first purple, then red, then both. Nobody would ever accuse Jim Bob of being uppity!

"We have a gentleman here who needs to see you. He came to us with some wild story about smuggling. We'll leave him to talk to you."

"Now wait one fuckin' minute here. . . ." But the two men were gone without further comment.

"Those fellas aren't FBI."

"No, sir, they're not. I hired them to bring me out here. Seems you're a hard man to see."

"I got an office for that. See me there!"

"Peter Coy Booker." Steven Dye said it with no preamble and no explanation.

"What?" The man's attention was definitely piqued.

"I said, Peter Coy Booker."

"Man's dead."

75

"Nope, he's not." Steven Dye pushed his way into the man's house, compounding his legal infractions since leaving Miami. He was strung out on uppers, trying to stay awake to find the goddamn boat.

"You can't come into my house like that, son. Now you best leave, and I won't call the police."

"You just have to tell me whatever you know about a boat built for Booker in ninety-one."

The man walked to a bar, poured two fingers of sour mash bourbon into each of two glasses, and handed one to Steven Dye.

"Wait here. I'll get dressed. But you're wasting your time. Booker's dead."

Jim Bob Jackson was a man of big appetites, including two women, both of whom he introduced as his wife.

"One ain't enough for a man like me," he said. "Had three, once. Don't know where she's gone off to. Took my pink Caddy and a few thousand dollars and ran off with a cabin boy. Beat's all."

"Mr. Jackson, I just came from Miami where I talked to a man named Andy. He says he made sails for a boat you built. Now I find out you don't build boats. What exactly *do* you do?"

"I'm a pirate."

"I beg your pardon?"

"Just a little joke, son. I design 'em, and I sail 'em. And sometimes, like when Mr. Booker asked, I carried supplies for him."

"Supplies . . . what kind?"

"Don't know. I never asked, and he never told me." One of his wives walked through the elaborately furnished room, so incongruous with its owner, so out of step as to be uncomfortable. Maybe he *was* a pirate, thought Steven. He must steal all this stuff. Wierd man. Wierd house. Steven pressed on.

"Did you design this boat?" Steven handed him the picture of Booker's sailboat.

"*The Assassin.*"

"What?"

"That's her name. *The Assassin.* Great little boat. Faster than most with plenty of room. Yeah, I designed her. Built most of her, too. Used the house yards, right next to the hourly folk. I'm not hourly folk."

Steven glanced around. No, he wasn't hourly folk.

"Did Booker pick it up?"

"Like I told you, Booker's dead."

"No, he's not. He's kidnapped a friend of mine. I'm going to find him, but I need help."

"I told you. Booker's dead. I can't help. Eyleah, get this boy another drink, so he . . ."

That's as much as he said and as far as he got before he found himself flat on his back with Steven Dye astride him like a cowboy riding a bull. But this cowboy had a 9 mm pressed tightly against Jim Bob's forehead. Jim Bob's eyes crossed comically as he stared at the barrel that rested lightly between his eyes.

"Now, son, you really oughtn't to get this upset so early in the morning. Gets your digestive tract all mussed up."

"Talk to me or I'll blow your pirate head off."

Jim Bob looked into Steven's eyes, saw the tiredness, saw the desperation to know, and imagined, most of all, a bullet exiting the gun and splashing his brains all over his Persian rug.

"You designed the boat?"

"Yes."

"You built it?"

"Most of it, yes."

"Booker didn't pick it up?"

"No."

"Who did?"

"Nobody."

"Nobody?"

"Right. I delivered it myself, to his place. Stayed three months, turned out."

Steven Dye pulled the gun away from the man's sweating forehead, put it back in its shoulder holster, and stood up. He extended his hand, and Jim Bob took it and got to his feet.

"Sorry, Jim Bob. I get excited when things don't seem to be going right, but now I'm excited because they *are* going right."

"I sailed *The Assassin* soon as she was seaworthy. After some trials off the coast, I took her straight to Booker's place."

"Where, exactly, *is* Booker's place?"

"Well, *The Assassin* has been all over the world since then, but I delivered her originally to a small island in the Caribbean, off the beaten path, you might say,"

"How far off the beaten path?"

"Completely out of the normal traffic lanes. You'd probably have to be lost to find it."

"Can you show me on a map?"

"Nope."

"Why not!" Steven's voice rose with impatience.

"Because, boy, it ain't on the map. Popped itself out of the ocean back in the twenties. The few people that visited it couldn't even find a place to moor their ships. Nice beach, but no fresh water. A fifteen-hundred-foot mountain with a narrow strip of flatland on three sides. One side is shear cliff to the sea. By 1950 or so, no one even bothered to chart it anymore."

"How did Peter Booker find it?"

"Well son, I know Mr. Peter Booker better than most. One of the reasons I'm alive is that I never asked him much. But he talked about what he did, sometimes. Come to find out his flying boat, you know, that relic from World War Two he travels in sometimes. . . ."

"Yes, I know, a Sannenson 80."

"Yeah, only one left. Anyway, it had engine trouble of some kind and planted itself right smack in front of that little island. Booker was stuck there for forty-eight hours. He went ashore, and then he left. The following year, Booker's seagoing tugs barged a construction crew to that island. He named it Predator Bay, and a year later, it had houses, a desalinization plant, power generators, dock, and enough firepower stored there to start a war on Haiti, which I believe he tried to do a time or two. I have aerial photos of it during construction. He hired me to sort of look after that part of it. I did good, so later, ten years later, he hired me to build the boat you're looking for and sail it to Predator Bay. That was in ninety-one. Never got a call back, never been back. With Booker dead, island's most likely gone all to hell."

"Booker's not dead, but I won't bore you with the details. Please pack up whatever information on Predator Bay you can find. Charts, maps, photos, snapshots, anything. Everything! Don't hold back a single thing that might make taking that island away from whoever's on it easier."

"And if I don't?" Jim Bob's face took on a hard and serious look. Steven Dye knew that Booker had few confidants in the world. He was pretty sure this man was one of them. He pulled the 9mm back out of his shoulder holster and attached a compact but effective silencer to it.

"Do as I say, or I'll kill you right now and find the stuff myself."

"That'll take days."

"True, but I'll be alive to waste time, won't I? You'll be dead."

"Booker will kill me."

"Not if *we* kill *him*."

"Hell, kid, you won't use that thing."

The gun shifted then fired once with a silent little "phfft" sound, and Jim Bob found himself knocked onto his back. He was bleeding from a clean flesh wound to the shoulder. He wouldn't die from that one, but he was seriously concerned with where the next shot might go.

"Okay." His two wives were already tending him, wrapping his bloody shoulder with a kitchen towel.

"Okay, what?"

"I'll do what you say, but you gotta take me with you until this is all over. I'm dead if you don't. You might just as well shoot me again if you won't cover my ass by taking me with you."

"Transportation can be arranged. I'll protect you as long as necessary. Just provide us with information about the island, and you can write your own ticket."

"One million dollars."

"I can't guarantee it, but if your stuff is as useful as it sounds like it is, I believe that's an acceptable deal." Steven Dye failed to mention that he had no authority whatsoever to make such a deal.

"Why, sonny, you just bought yourself a walking, talking, wounded encyclopedia."

Deal accepted, thought Steven. Where do you borrow a million dollars? He felt like Superman.

In thirty minutes, the house was stripped of Jim Bob's papers which required two large suitcases to carry. Jim Bob's shoulder was taped for temporary travel, and the two men and their bags were aboard a Marine twin-engine transport and airborne for Nellis AFB within two hours. Steven Dye finally got some sleep.

Nellis AFB, Hangar 21A
1:50 A.M. January 4, 1994

With the SCAR computer still at work accepting and digesting both old and new data on Booker's hideaway, one quarter-panel of hangar wall had been turned into a vast blackboard. Photo blowups of snapshots, construction photos, road and island resource data all began to pile up, completing a picture for the Confirmed Kill Team of an island shaped ominously like a skull and bristling with defensive positions. A large dock branched out from the "mouth" of the skull, and old photos showed it and all the other construction activity from start to finish. The wounded boat maker, now resting in the 21A medical facility, had earned his million, and more. Information on the island was as complete as if it had been done by a Coast Guard survey.

"It's the mother lode, I'd say," said Penelope James, standing near the wall, her slim frame dwarfed by the display and its intelligence riches.

"Isn't it, though? But there's one thing missing from all this information," Michael Barns said with a frown.

"Really? What might that be, Michael?"

"How to take this island without getting Maggie killed in the process. That's the kind of information we can only get ashore. Clearly she's in one of the houses. They're close to the boat and at the end of the road from the airstrip. Good beach, good dock, tropical paradise, but we still don't have enough information to guarantee her rescue."

"And the senator's," said Steven.

"Yeah, of course, but I'll tell you right now, Maggie's the first priority. Delta Force won't be far behind on this information. They've got every intelligence satellite possible at work. I figure we have a twelve-hour window to get in and get out with Maggie. The truth is, I don't see a safe way to do it. We may kill Maggie. I don't want to put her at more risk than she already is."

Con Duggan walked past the group of teammates and intelligence-types and affixed eight Polaroid photos to the wall. He turned around to face them, his face gray with worry and stress.

"Look at these, and look real good. We go as soon as we decide the safest way. My target is tomorrow at zero-four-hundred island time. Try to figure a way to do it—we've got to hurry."

He walked back through the group and boarded the 21A transport aircraft, the black-painted C-130 that had carried them so dependably on past missions.

"Where's he going?"

"To bed, I think," Michael said. "Look at those pictures like he said."

"Oh . . . oh my God," Penelope whispered, her body swaying as she realized the Polaroids were of Maggie's rape, in graphic detail.

The team didn't dwell on the photos and instantly developed a feeling of collective protectiveness for Maggie's violated state.

"We're too bloody late!" Penelope lamented.

"No—she's had a rough time, but she's not dead. I'm sure of that. This is typical of Booker. He wants us to charge at him like undisciplined idiots, but we won't do that. I don't want any heroics here—no *revenge for Maggie* stuff!" Michael stopped to collect his thoughts before going on, fixing each member of the team with his relentlessly professional gaze. Whatever he felt about the rape photos, not a trace of those feelings rose to the surface. His job was to support and direct the Confirmed Kill Team's missions, and, his long friendship with Con Duggan and Maggie notwithstanding, that's what he intended to do.

"Right about now, General Cassidy and his Delta group are beginning to sort out *their* information from Defense Department satellites. Steven and Penelope got lucky, thank God! It's reliably reported by a friend in the White House that Cassidy has ID'd the location of Booker's little paradise and has ordered high-level, high-speed reconnaissance aircraft to photograph it. Figure a six-hour mission on the photos, six more to interpret them, and then however good Cassidy is at strike-planning determines how fast he moves. We know his attack unit consists of one twenty-eight–man SEAL unit and an elite airborne commando unit. We have a twelve-hour start, but he could hit anytime after that. I believe he'll assault the beach from the sea with small boats released by submarine mother ships already en route. By air, they'll probably drop a six- to ten-man hit team. What all this means, I believe, is that if we don't hit them at zero-four-hundred tomorrow, the Delta team will be there by zero-*six*-hundred. If they get there first, Maggie's as good as dead, along with most of the Delta team. They're brave but led by a 20th Century Custer. We've got to keep our emotions under control and direct *all* our efforts to saving Mags first, and then getting off that island before the Delta team arrives.

"Understand, people, that if we fail, the continued existence of this unit is doubtful. We *must* pull it off—and in a way the President of the United States can deal with politically. Right now, begin to prepare yourself for the most dangerous mission this or any other clandestine unit has ever attempted. We'll have to be at our best." Here, he paused, his features softening a bit.

"Nap time, now . . . it's zero-three-hundred. I want you down for six hours. We hit Predator Bay, with or without a good plan, at zero-four-hundred tomorrow, January fifth. Hard to believe isn't it? Only five days ago, we were all at a party together, toasting the New year. Now get some rest—maybe we can finish the party tomorrow."

10

"Black Bird Two to Station."

"Go, Blackbird Two."

"I'm at eighty-thousand feet, commencing high-speed photo run on target designate . . . Island A."

"Roger, Blackbird Two. We need four runs north-south, four runs east-west, and one oblique run to focus on cliffs."

Back at his Delta unit headquarters, General Cassidy tapped his fingers impatiently, waiting for the two sleek, updated SR-71 Blackbird aircraft to complete their part of his mission to rescue the senator. He was monitoring the planes and had the capability to communicate with them which he did from time to time.

"Blackbird 1A, commencing east-west."

"Roger, 1A."

"Blackbird Two also commencing east-west."

"Roger, Two.

Cassidy turned to his operations officer, barely able to contain his enthusiasm, "Now, goddamnit, Colonel, we're almost there! Pictures only a few hours away. Tomorrow, Delta Force can rock and roll!" General Cassidy was a happy Ceasar.

"Yes, sir. The support submarine is en route. The skipper reports expected arrival time two miles northeast of Predator Bay is twenty-one hundred hours tomorrow. Will signal for team injection onto sub by air."

"Right! Damn, I'm the captain of a team that's red hot! Here we come, Senator." The radio crackled, and Cassidy returned his attention to it.

"Blackbird Two?"

"This is Blackbird Two, go ahead."

"I show red light, repeat red light, on camera-bay panel. Camera two malfunction. Will try to restart."

"Restart that thing, goddamnit!" General Cassidy was nearly in a panic at the thought that this recon flight might not get all the information he wanted.

"Doing my best, General. Restart procedure initiated."

There was a long pause.

"Red light continues. Camera malfunction confirmed. Detail shots doubtful if warning light is accurate."

"Take the fucking pictures anyway!" Cassidy's face was turning red with frustration.

"But, General, I . . ."

"Do it!" Cassidy's voice rose to a high-pitched wail.

"Read you loud and clear, station. Run with red-lighted camera. Is that what you're saying, sir?"

"Damn straight!"

"Heard and understood, station. Commencing camera run number one, north-south at eighty K."

"Blackbird 1A, east-west initial run completed. Camera system green. Commencing second run, north-south."

"Well, at least one of them is doing the fucking job," mumbled the general as he monitored the Florida-based spy planes.

The super-secret craft, traveling at three times the speed of sound, could photograph a bite out of a cookie from eighty thousand feet. From that lofty height came a startled voice, professional, but excited.

"May Day, May Day! This is Blackbird 1A! Explosion in aircraft bay! Fire light red, alarm on! Smoke from unknown source in cockpit! Blackbird 1A aborting photo mission and returning to base!"

"Wait! Goddamit, finish your job first!" General Cassidy overrode the pilot's request for further flight instructions until an Air Force general told him in no uncertain terms to temporarily get off the airwaves, so they could initiate emergency operations. Fire was a pilot's deadliest fear.

"All right. Blackbird Two, you take over all the runs."

"General Cassidy, this is Blackbird Two. Orders received and will cover *all* photo lanes for mission number 1066. Camera still red-lighted on forward bay. Only one camera green. Well, General?"

"Fly it! Maybe the light's out of order."

"Received and understood. Two out."

"Covering his ass."

"What'd you say, Colonel?"

"The pilot of Blackbird Two. Covering his ass for flying a quarter-million-dollar mission with a down camera."

"Let him cover it. I don't give a fuck!"

Delta Force Headquarters
11:00 A.M. January 4, 1994

"General, we have the results of the two-plane photo mission you ordered."

"Go, Colonel."

"The red light was correct. Only one forward camera functioned on Blackbird Two. We have half of two thousand photographs. It's like having one tit to look at. Interesting, but you can't see the whole situation. The 1A aircraft landed safely. A tire blew in the wheel-closure area. No fire, just tire smoke. Still, it showed as a fire. They had to disengage the damn bell alarm after he got back okay. Nearly drove the pilot nuts."

"So where do we stand?"

"Where we were before the mission started. Both birds have to go back. The cameras are okay now, the tires are fixed. They're cleared to re-fly the mission. Otherwise, we got zip."

"Send 'em off. This time, you monitor them. They cost me ten hours for nothing. Tell 'em I want the job done right this time."

"Yes, sir."

"How about the SEAL's submarine operation?"

"On schedule, sir."

"Well, something's going right."

"Yes, sir. We'll get them, sir."

"Who?"

"Why the senator and his daughter, sir."

"Oh, yeah. Of course we will. Piece o' cake."

"I'll tell the White House we're on schedule then?"

"Better tell them the truth. We've suffered a slight setback timewise, but tell them we'll deliver a United States Senator tomorrow night."

"Don't forget the daughter."

"Right. The daughter . . ."

"Well, they were worth the effort, after all. Nice work! My compliments to the pilots. They'll receive commendations, of course. Tell them for me."

"Of course, General. They're very valuable photos."

"Okay. It's nineteen hundred hours. We've lost some time. By zero-one hundred hours, I want you team leaders, both sea and airborne, to come up with an assault plan with as much a guarantee as fate can provide that we spring the senator. Of course, I'm concerned about the Delta Force, but I want no consideration given to casualties. Delta will undoubtedly take some. How many, I can't predict, but low casualty figures are likely *if* the time element is favorable. We know the senator's there. We know Booker, or whatever his name is, has him. We must assume the island has some defensive soldiers on it, but probably not more than six or eight. None of this can be further confirmed, so we go in hot and shooting when shot at. Or, for that matter, if you *think* you might get shot at."

Here the commander of Delta Force gave them what he hoped was a meaningful look. "Okay, air drop by parachute, sea landing by powered rubber boat. Give me a plan I can launch within four-hours' notice from 'go' to execution. Complete the initial SEAL para-drop to the sub at the earliest. We should be able to do that as soon as the Navy is on station off Predator Bay. The final 'go' is at zero-one-hundred. Dismissed!"

Aboard the Sea Dragon *in the Caribbean* 10:00 P.M. January 4, 1994

The submarine slid to the surface, its hull black but sparkling with thousands of sequin-like organisms native to Caribbean waters. Nearly silent, the ship moved slowly on the surface in a mile-wide circle, blacked out topside except for a special signal light that could be seen only from the air. The exercise about to commence had been done many times before in training but not during the hours of darkness. The moon was out, but a shifting cover of huge, fluffy clouds stalked by it one after the other to keep the night darker than usual.

The captain of the sub, a slim, humorless type, a perfect fit for the clandestine operation, swept the periscope around in two full circles. Nothing.

"Radar?"

"Clear, Cap'n. Just that ole island two miles off. Somebody play'n some kind of wierd Oriental music that I'm pickin' up on the mikes. Sure ain't no country boy."

"At least from *this* country, you mean."

"Golly, that's a good one, Cap'n. I liked that."

The captain's grin showed his even white teeth in the red-lit periscope deck. The cornpone talk of his veteran seventeen-year radar/sonar chief hid the man's master's degree in engineering. The pig boat was crawling with nerdy, but nervy, crewmen drawn from all over the service. The captain thought his crew was superb, if not quite balanced. The sub and the Delta equipment it carried was a boy's ultimate Nintendo game. They had done some dark deeds now and then, but nothing to top this.

"Message from aircraft, sir."

"Verify."

"They are verified, sir. Delta SMI aircraft twelve-man drop, request drop lights six minutes from . . . *now*."

"Mark!"

"Mark six minutes, Captain. Preliminary switches on, timer activated. Aircraft forty miles and closing at eight hundred feet."

"Keep a close watch, Bonney."

"Will do, sir."

"Red lights in sequence, on. Hook-up. Go on green-system switch, four minutes."

The plane's rear ramp swung out and down, a kind of slide for the twelve-man SEAL team. Even though one of its men was a woman, the CO referred to everyone as "man." She didn't seem to mind, though.

"That tub of tin better be there," a team member groused.

"What's-a matter, Willy boy? You scared of the dark?"

"Damn straight. Hate jumpin' too. Hate the water even more."

"Then goddamn, Willy, *why* are you in this outfit?"

"Beats me all to hell. Right now, I'd rather be in Paduka."

"Why? Ain't nothing in Paduka."

"My girl."

"I've seen her picture. You're better off jumpin' out of airplanes. I wouldn't fuck that girl with a stick. Oops! Excuse me, Brenda."

Their female team member just winked her acceptance. She had long since quit being offended. Brenda Starr was her name, just like the girl in the comics. She figured she was destined to be surrounded by rough men with hard muscles and big dicks. Well, two of them anyway.

"Three minutes. Chest hook check. Move to the door."

"Two minutes. On the ramp to the yellow lines."

"One minute—one minute! We go on full green light."

"Still wish I was back in Paduka."

"Full green! Go, go, *go!*" The ramp was empty of the team and its two rubber boats in less than five seconds. The door swung back and closed, and the aircraft pulled away from the drop zone. Twenty-two minutes later, the *Sea Dragon* picked them up safely and slid back into the sea. Part of General Cassidy's commando unit was on station and ready to assault the island when ordered. It was 2300 hours, and they settled in to await the go signal. It was the first night drop in the team's history. The general promised commendations all around.

On Predator Bay, Booker's sophisticated Russian radar, bootlegged out of Eastern Europe for $100,000 cash in '92, displayed the whole operation and provided Booker with accurate information, including the last whereabouts of the sub and the fact that it had received an airdrop of some kind. He knew immediately that this was not Con Duggan. Whoever it was would not have much success against his tight little island. He was aware, but not yet concerned. He could escape the island at a moment's notice and take his bait with him. The assault from the sea would result only in dead rescuers.

Nellis AFB, Hangar 21A
3:00 P.M. January 4, 1994

"Okay, team, we have a plan, such as it is, so we'll go over it one more time."

"God, Michael, not again!"

"Penelope, are you absolutely confident you understand the mission, and that you, personally, are totally prepared?"

"Bloody right."

"How much 40-cal is aboard the *Whisper?* How much 30? Are the complete range of gun components for the SIKIM aboard?"

"Well, I . . . I think so."

"Check it again!" said Michael in a stern voice, that of an angry uncle.

"Yes, Michael," she replied, her voice small and obedient.

Ivan Tescher, the *Whisper's* dauntless pilot, walked to the vast intelligence display taped and tacked to the hangar wall and stopped in front of a six-foot blown-up photo of the island taken from the air by Jim Bob shortly after the house was completed. Some of the red-tiled roof had yet to be laid, and only the dark crisscrossing of setup braces showed on about a third of the roof. Still, the photo displayed the island's installations and housing in vivid detail. Sixty smaller, individual section photos from the larger island photo and photo packs of intended or possible targets had been distributed to all concerned.

"For our purposes here today, we'll use the island's natural and unusual skull shape to point out possible resistance, definite resistance, and natural hazards.

"The island's top, the 'head' area on the skull, is a two-hundred-fifty to fifteen-hundred-foot mountainous cliff facing north. The beach at the base of the cliff wall, as you can see, is hardly worth the name. No landing is possible there, and we will not use the cliffs to get at the south beach, where the large house and dock facilities are. Try to follow along in your imagination as we fly the approach the *Whisper* will take sometime after 0400 hours tomorrow."

Ivan took another sip from his coffee mug before he addressed the Confirmed Kill Team. Then he said, "We will approach Predator Bay from dead north, if you'll excuse the expression. As a pilot, I don't like this mission very much, and here's why. We'll sort of pop up, like toast, over the cliff and immediately dive into the southern 'eye' of the skull, the deep depression you see in the darkened area of the photo. There are two of these jungle 'holes' in the island. Probably, nobody's in there. It looks like about two-thirds of a mile of dense brush. While we're in there, we hope we'll remain unnoticed and receive no hostile fire." He drained the coffee in one slug, wrinkling his nose in distaste.

"As you can clearly see in the photo, the island support installations are built right out in the open, with access cleared to the little dirt road the island has. Only jeeps on it, it seems, and we can see five in the picture. At each end of the runway and on the road to the beach are guard towers. Here and here," he said, tapping the photo with a pointer, "with another tower by the generator station. We have to assume they're manned 'round the clock. I'll take the generator and its tower down on the way to the beach drop. Now I'll let Michael take it from there." Without another word, the *Whisper* pilot sat down, lighting the remainder of a cigar stub and staring intently at the toes of his boots.

"Thanks, Ivan. Succinct, as always.

"Okay, the mad Russian has shot up the generator and a guard tower, risking life, limb, and the mighty *Whisper*, and we find ourselves on a white-sand beach under the brightly shining stars. From here on, our plan fails to live up to its name. Basically, we expect to be engaged by gunfire of some type from both beach towers and possibly the dock as well. Steven and Penelope will exit the *Whisper* and direct SIKIM 1000 fire at whatever targets of opportunity seem most appropriate. After the towers are suppressed, Steven is to occupy one and shoot at any targets that appear. Penelope, with her street-sweeper shotgun, is to then join me and Con Duggan at the main house.

"Ivan will clear the beach as soon as the beach-drop personnel are in motion toward their objectives. He will then go airborne again and provide whatever firepower he can when requested. He'll return to the beach *only* when ordered back by an identifiable teammate. If all goes as planned, we'll fly out of there for Chrystal Island, a navy research base, 177 miles north of Booker's little fortress on the sea. We'll fly the *Whisper* over water directly to the Predator Bay strike zone, carry out our tasks, return to the navy station, and finally be back home here in twenty-four hours.

"If we're not back here by 1600 hours tomorrow with a safe Maggie, it will be assumed we've failed in our mission, and that we are all most likely dead. This isn't really a plan, more like a street rumble between two gangs, a street fight, with Maggie as the turf. We go there and kill anybody who has her. That's the plan, what there is of it. Con, you got anything you want to add to this incredibly sophisticated operation I've laid out here?"

"Yup, a little. First of all, try to keep control of yourself when we hit the island. You younger team members—"

"You mean Steven Yank and me, Con Duggan!"

"Yes, I do, Penelope. We really don't know what to expect, but we've got to keep one goal in mind: Maggie, Maggie, Maggie. Don't go off into the jungle shooting up bad guys unless you have to. Michael and I are going right to the house. Penelope, you have to extinguish beach opposition and join us as quickly as you can. And remember, if we get lucky, we'll get to her *before* Delta Force arrives. If not, we'll have to deal with General Cassidy.

"Maggie, she's our goal—everything else is secondary. Don't endanger her life to save her! If somebody's got the drop on you, back off. We can get her killed, if we're not *steady*. Keep that in mind. Two more thoughts: Keep your cool under stress, and get to Maggie. Otherwise, it's all for nothing. One way or another, the President will be mad at the Confirmed Kill Team—that's the only sure thing about this whole mission. In my heart, I know you'll all do your duty—to this team, to this family."

And then Con Duggan wiped at his eyes and headed deeper into the hangar, toward the C-130.

"Questions?" asked Michael. There were none, only the unspoken fear that this was a totally crazy plan that couldn't possibly work.

The Delta plan, an airdrop and a combined assault from the *Sea Dragon's* SEAL team, was finally approved and scheduled for 0600 5 January. A stuck cargo door on the operation aircraft altered the time to 0730 island time. Basically, the order was simple. Officially, rescue the senator and his daughter. Unofficially, rescue the senator *first,* and have a high body count of bad guys and plenty of ready-to-sign commendations. There was a total air/sea Delta contingent of forty-one men and one woman. As Cassidy said before boarding a fast destroyer that evening, his team was "red hot." He notified the President that Delta Force would begin rescue operations at 0730 in the morning.

The Confirmed Kill Team was informed almost simultaneously of these plans by its source in the White House. The President knew about this conduit of information and allowed it. He was counting on Con Duggan to disobey his order. Later there would be forgiveness, or jail time, depending on the result.

11

The objects of all this activity were at a kind of truce: Maggie, calm and defiant; the senator taking it as a vacation, complete with lax sexual mores; and Booker, satisfied now that the bait was well set in his trap. From various sources he had cultivated over the decades, Booker knew with certainty that his island had been identified and slated for attack.

Soon, Con Duggan would be here to rescue his soiled paramour, the fairytale white charger probably changed now into a boat or parachute drop. He believed the assault, in whatever form, would begin the following morning after daybreak. He was right to an extent. Delta Force was scheduled to hit him then. What he didn't know was that Con Duggan would be there first, in the dark. But he felt prepared in any case.

Booker's objective was the personal destruction of the man who had nearly killed him in the waters off Folkestone, England, leaving him a bloody, burned hulk of a man that took two million dollars and fifteen months to put right. Now the burning hatred he felt for Con Duggan had settled to a steadily banked fire, a guiding hate that could only end with Con Duggan's death.

There were sixty heavily armed and well-trained mercenaries at Predator Bay, the best you could buy. They couldn't flee if in trouble, so they'd have to stand and fight, giving Booker plenty of time and opportunity to do his business

95

and escape on the cigarette boat tied up on the other side of the island, a short jeep ride away.

Out at sea, forty miles away, his headquarters boat, the *Isadora*, rocked gently at anchor, 102 feet of refuge, crewed, fueled, and ready to return him to the Mediterranean. Whatever the results of the tumult soon to visit the island, Booker could leave it whenever he wished. The cigarette boat, as fast as any drug running craft, was a ticket for one. He cared not a whit for the remainder of his men. If they survived, fine; if not, so be it.

He gazed seaward, tapping his new leather hand rhythmically against a deck chair aboard the *Assassin*.

"The rape was unnecessary, Peter." The usually silent Chin's voice was surprisingly soft, almost sweet for a man of his size and sheer physicality.

"I disagree. Raping the senator, raping the girl—gives them something to share. Consider it a gesture to reconcile a dysfunctional father/daughter relationship."

"You humiliate the father with the young woman and her constant physical demands on him."

"You approved earlier. Keeps him busy and out of the way."

"You did not reach the daughter. Maggie Stewart is made of stronger steel. You only serve her need to kill you."

"Good. I want her to hate me."

"Not hate, need. You have made her calm, and that will cost us. I feel it."

"You talk like an old woman, Chin! What the bloody hell is wrong with you?"

"This is not good. We should leave. Kill them if you must, but we should leave."

"I want Duggan."

"You call me an old woman, while you, Peter, have gone finally, truly mad." The massive Chin stood up and gracefully vaulted over the deck rail onto the dock. When he turned to face Booker, he found himself staring down the barrel of Booker's pistol.

"You won't shoot me, Peter."

"Really, now. And why won't I?"

"Because I'm the only human being you know who doesn't fear you. You need me, your curious occidental/oriental thought process needs me. I am your interpreter to the rest of the human race. Who else could translate your mad schemes?"

Booker lowered the gun slowly and finally slid it back into its waistband holster.

"That's true. Unfortunate, but true. Go check on your animals, Chin. See that they're fat and sleek for their executions."

Without another word, Chin walked away, his back a broad but psychologically unshootable target.

Booker sat back with a thump into the deck chair as a silent Pakistani steward refilled his drink. It always amazed him, this capacity for alcohol. What, he wondered, separated his apparent immunity from the senator's dependence on nearly everything. Sex, booze, power—fuel for a man with no insides, an inflatable man, hiding the air plug behind pompous good tidings at country fairs. Yet here, in two days, Booker had found that plug and pulled it, leaving the senator exposed to his true nature. And a sad, worthless nature it was. How, he thought, could a man that weak father a daughter so strong?

People were either strong or weak, and Booker had learned long ago that both traits could be exploited. He was now playing directly into Con Duggan's strengths, making the man weak and vulnerable in the process. A thinking man would never attempt a rescue under these circumstances. Didn't Duggan realize that at the first shot he, Booker, would draw the lovely Maggie to his side? Would Duggan shoot? How much would he risk? How much would he beg? How low would he bend? Delicious thoughts, dwelled on by a madman in the Caribbean sun.

Nellis AFB, Hangar 21A
4:00 P.M. January 4, 1994

Steven Dye watched as Penelope James puttered about their small quarters with its army-issue cots jammed together to form a haphazard double bed. The walls were concrete, and braided throw rugs from a Las Vegas K-Mart covered nearly every inch of the floor. Penelope rarely wore shoes at "home," and even with the rugs, the floor made her feet cold. So they'd spent very little time on base since the team had returned from its first mission, preferring an apartment they'd found behind a casino in downtown Vegas that Penelope decorated in sixties hippie style. Now, however, they were forced to occupy the small room inside Hanger 21A.

Time was short on this frantic attempt to find and rescue Maggie, so the entire team had either been on the road or staying at the spartan 21A Hangar, sleeping in quarters or in the vast open area under or next to a variety of aircraft. In effect, what quarters there were inside 21A were concrete boxes with bath and bed. Much of the available space contained the occupants' personnel weaponry.

The 25-million-dollar SIKIM-1000, supergun of the clandestine world, leaned against the wall of Steven and Penelope's room as casually as a 30-30 rifle. Occasionally, Penelope dried her undies by stretching a line from the gun to the bathroom doorknob. Home was where you hung your crotchless panties.

"Steven Yank?" Penelope said as she fidgeted. Waiting wreaked havoc with her nerves.

"Yeah?"

"Will Booker have a lot of shooters with him on Predator Bay?"

"We have no true count, you know that."

She turned away from the sink, popped two white-and-green capsules into her mouth, and washed them down with a glass of water and a casual toss of her head.

"I know. Just wondering."

Steven had stripped to the waist, preparing to shower. He sat on the lumpy bed and pulled off one of his boots. Rubbing his foot absently, he looked at her face, and it showed stress and lack of sleep around the lovely gray eyes. She leaned back against the sink, slowly rubbing the water glass back and forth on her forhead, head bent forward a little, black hair cascading over her shoulders and across her full breasts, too full, really, for her slim figure. She was dressed in a cammy top and shorts, with heavy socks and boots, and still managed somehow to look completely wanton and sexual. Steven felt himself harden and rise, poking up at the half unbuttoned jeans he wore.

"Are you scared, baby?"

"Some. I'm not usually scared, but this is so much different. This looks pretty much like a straightforward military assault, and I'm not much for the idea."

"If you have reservations, Penelope, you should tell Con Duggan."

As sometimes happened, the volatile woman inside Penelope's psyche burst loose and went off in his face. "Oh, bloody yes, let's tell the bereaved and desperate Con Duggan I don't like his non-plan one little bit! I can hear it now from the commissary to the medical wards! 'Only a matter o' time, wasn't it? The sexy little Brit can't handle it! It's just a little island in paradise. What's she worried about, then? The Brits lost their fucking empire, now she wants to lose ours!' You know bloody well I can't say anything!"

"You can withdraw from the mission, Penelope."

"No, I can't. Not any more than you or Con or Michael can. It's Maggie, after all, and he's raped her! I've been raped, lots of times. Maggie's tough, tough as me, I think, or Con wouldn't love her like he does." Her voice softened and the sudden volatility faded away.

"Do you love me, Steven?" She had set the glass aside, and her hands rested against the sink, her arms bent at the elbows, supporting her body with her feet stretched out together in front of her. She looked about fourteen years old at that moment. She was older than he was, chronologically and in many other ways, but right now, she seemed like a child during an afternoon recess from school.

Steven removed his other boot, then the sock. He stood and pulled his pants off, then sat down in his Jockey shorts, looking at her. What did she want here? he wondered.

"I asked you if you loved me, Steven."

"You know I do."

"Really? How? How do I know that?"

"We're good together."

"In bed, you mean?"

"Well, that's part of it, yes."

"We *are* good together, I'll admit, though you have much to learn and I have much to teach you. Still, that doesn't tell me why you love me. That tells me you love my body. Fine. I'm pleased. But there must be more."

"What are you looking for?"

"An answer. Do you love me?"

"Yes, I told you!" Exasperated now, he stood up and pulled an icy beer from the small fridge.

"Would you miss me if I was gone?"

"Immeasurably."

"Ahh . . . good word that. Do I delight you in all I do?"

"Yes, you delight me in all you do."

"You lie!"

"Yes, I lie."

"Would you say anything at this moment to placate me?"

"Yes."

"Then perhaps you really do love me. Go take your bloody shower."

He waited for her to say more, but she turned away. He'd been dismissed. He dropped his underwear and headed for the bathroom and its modern shower.

Steam filled the bathroom, and the water, hot as he could bear, lashed at him. Steven considered what she'd said and decided it was indecipherable female gibberish. Then the door opened, admitting a sharp blast of air-conditioned coolness. The steam escaped for a moment, but quickly built up again. He sensed her enter the shower behind him, and then her hands snaked their way around his hips and down the front of him, to his cock, and she began to pull and stroke at it, her large breasts pressed against his narrow back.

"All those martial arts you do—where are your muscles?" Penelope's voice was demure and teasing now.

"Don't have any and don't need any. Martial arts are for extreme conditions when I need to kill with speed and cunning, not muscles."

Her mouth, close to his, whispered and tongued him at the same time. "This is a muscle, this grows. Watch it grow, watch it get bigger. . . ." And then she slid around in front of him and grasped his dick, raging hard now and straining, his knees bent slightly as she gazed up at him, the shower lashing her head and his groin as she wrapped her slim hands tightly around him, her mouth held near, but not touching him, eyes looking into his through a fog of hot water and steam.

"Do you want me to suck it? Do you? Tell me what you want."

"Yes."

"Yes, what, Steven Yank?" Her voice sounded raw and shaky, and through the steam, he could see her tugging viciously at one of her nipples, always large and full, now like raw dates as she twisted them and rubbed them against the head of his penis, the nipple battering at the small hole.

"Tell me, Steven—tell me what you want."

"Suck me. Please, honey, suck me."

"What, Steven—suck what?"

"My cock! Suck my cock!"

At that response, her mouth covered him and slid along like molten steel, all alive and hot until she had buried her lips against the pubic hair of his crotch. After a long, exquisite moment, she pulled her lips away, slowly, then all the way back, her eyes tiny slits of heat locked on his. She enveloped him into her mouth again and down her throat this time, deeper than he had believed possible. This was something new, something she'd saved until now. Then she pulled her mouth free of him, and with her hand, held his cock against his stomach as she sucked his balls into her mouth, first one at a time, then both, her hand stroking him, faster and faster. She sat back on her haunches and finished him, using both hands, his semen arcing out in jets and landing on her face, where she let it sit, making no attempt to wash it off, her hands directing it down her body like massage cream, until it had vanished into the pores of her skin. Finally she stood up, turned her back to him, and thrust her face into the shower only inches from the spray's hardest concentration.

She leaned her head back, drew his mouth to hers, and kissed him, sort of upside down, as the water continued to batter at them. Then she pulled the shower curtain back, looked at him with an expression too mystical for him to decipher, and stepped out. His shaky legs no longer able to support him, he sat down in the shower, the water hitting the wall behind him. He felt muscleless, strengthless, a rag doll. He didn't know whether to be happy or terrified about what had just happened to him.

Finally he got out of the shower and began to dry off, his mind blank. Like much of what she did, he knew that it was important for her to have done it. And like much of what she did, he didn't truly understand it. She was a witch, and he was the bewitched. For now, that was enough.

While two of the younger members of the Confirmed Kill Team dealt with their anxieties one way, Michael and Con sat quietly aboard the 21A–C-130 while technicians scurried about the big aircraft, making it flight-ready and secure.

The lower ramp was down, the nose was up, and the specially fitted aircraft was nearly loaded for the mission. The helicopter, fueled up, as it had been for the bullet train assault in Japan, had been brought aboard without complication and secured for flight. The flight plan included one stop for refueling, at Hempstead AFB in Florida, on to the navy base on Chrystal Island, then the final 177 miles to Predator Bay. Timing was important, but not critical to mission success—they had a two-hour attack window, between 0400 and 0600, but the closer to 0400, the better.

"The plan stinks, Con," Michael said with a dejected air.

"Naw, it just hasn't got anything to do with reality. Otherwise, it's a wonderful plan."

"Yeah, typical for this team, I guess. I keep expecting a white rabbit to appear proclaiming how late he is."

"You said that exact thing when we were in England."
There was a note of challenge in Con's voice.

"Did I? Yes, I probably did. It fit there and it fits here.
Hell, all the shit aboard this plane won't help us one whit on
that fucking island. If he decides to kill Maggie the minute
we hit him, there isn't a damn thing we can do about it."

"True, but he won't do that."

"Why not?"

"Because he wants to kill *me,* not Maggie. Maggie, bless
her, is the tethered lamb. I'm the beast that's supposed to
go after it. He may kill her, yes, but not until he has to.
He wants me to come to him, and when I do, he'll have
Maggie with him."

"Well, you can't do it, that's all."

"Can't do what?"

"Just go right to him like that."

"I have to if I want her alive."

"Maybe we'll get lucky."

"Don't hold your breath."

The two men looked at each other with complete
understanding. They had a not-very-good plan against a
dug-in, resourceful maniac who was hell-bent for revenge.
Even bad luck would be more luck than they expected.

"The kids," Con said somewhat uncertainly.

"Yeah, they'll have to grow all the way up on this
trip."

"They're pretty good. Let's hope we don't get them pretty
dead as well."

"Angels can't do more," Michael told him.

They were scheduled to leave Nellis at 2215 hours. Time
to rest, but the two men played game after game of cribbage
instead. By 2200 hours, Con was ahead by $26.00.

12

"Tower, this is 21A–C-130. Request permission to approach taxiway."

"Already, 21A? Don't like our service, huh?"

"Service is fine, Tower. Request permission to approach taxiway!"

His attempt at humor rejected, the tower man got down to business. "Granted, 21A. Taxiway request okay. Free to taxi on access."

"Roger, Tower. Free to taxi on access. 21A received."

Standing in the well space between the pilot and copilot, Con Duggan stared into the darkness as the aircraft rocked slightly on its wings and headed toward the takeoff point. "Nice job gettin' us here, boys," he said.

"Thanks, Con, but now we gotta find that little navy island in the Atlantic, only a hip-hop from the Caribbean . . . My kid loves maps. He was talking the other day about the South Atlantic and the Caribbean. He wanted to know how you could tell them apart when they're right up against each other. I told him one was an ocean, the other a sea."

"And?"

"And I was stuck right there. Good thing he's only five."

105

"You ever marry that woman, Carl?"

"Helen? Naw. We been together twenty-nine years. Why fuck up a good thing?" It was like that on this trip. A lot of small talk, hiding the fears, moving into the line. No matter how sophisticated the Confirmed Kill Team's combat might be, to Con Duggan, it was all the same. The other guy was still trying to kill him.

"I told 'em we were gonna run some navigational test, Con, so when we fly south over water, they won't be surprised none."

"Fine, Carl. Just set us down on that research island. You got enough runway to land there?"

"Sort of. It's about a thousand feel less what this bird is supposed to need at this weight, but we'll do it anyway."

"Michael will be on the ground with me after we deploy. Michelle will handle communications this time."

"Michelle? Pretty young, pretty inexperienced." The pilot looked dubious.

"Did you ever get a close look at Steven Dye and Penelope James, Carl?"

"I see what you mean."

"Fine. Just fly when and where she tells you."

"No problem, Con. Don't worry, this old bird will be wherever you want it to be."

"Tower, where's that clearance? Runnin' late here, pard."

"Received, 21A–C-130. Permission to fly when you're ready. Have a nice trip."

"Thanks, Tower. See ya." Without any fuss the C-130 picked up speed while still on the taxiway and swung onto the runway at nearly takeoff speed. The team cleared the ground at 0259 hours, still within the mission's operational window and on the early side. Early was good.

As they circled back over the base, they picked up a request to land from what their onboard SCAR computer identified as a transport aircraft assigned to Delta Force. "Cassidy's paras, I'll bet," Con Duggan speculated. "Direct flight to the island from Homestead. Daylight drop. Without us in there first, he'd probably land a shot-dead paratroop assault team."

Aboard the Cossack, Caribbean Sea
3:00 A.M. January 5, 1994

Cassidy stood on the deck of the British destroyer *Cossack*, borrowed, so to speak, while on a Caribbean good-will jaunt with a royal or two aboard. The royals had been quickly offloaded in Jamaica, and now the *Cossack's* captain wanted to offload the obnoxious senior officer standing like a Caesar on his deck.

"They should surface soon, sir. We're on station."

"You've contacted them?"

"Yes, General. They should be right below us." And, indeed, they were. The *Sea Dragon* rose splashily to the surface and ran alongside the *Cossack* while a rubber-boat transfer was made between the two ships. General Cassidy was now officially in position, and he immediately messaged the President to inform him of that fact.

True, he was aboard a submarine, and so were his SEAL assault troops, along with a ten-man Marine SEAL contingent that was aboard the *Sea Dragon* at all times. They would join him. These men and their commander declared themselves ready at 0300 hours, while the actual assault, scheduled to coincide with the airdrop, was still four and a half hours distant.

The Confirmed Kill Team would hit the island long before that. Still, Delta Force was two and a half miles from its target and "on station" as reported. The White House response was less than overwhelming.

The communications station at Predator Bay monitored all of this sea activity. Booker was not alarmed. He entered Maggie's quarters without knocking and found her sitting quietly on the couch, having a drink of brandy and reading a book.

"Ah, you're up."

"How astute of you, Booker."

"I shall ignore your disrespect. After all, I courted that attitude. We shall soon have visitors. Ships of the mighty and the righteous maneuver off our shores, even as we speak. They seem quite serious about rescuing you."

"Not me, my father."

"Oh, then you think this bunch isn't Con Duggan and his murderous cohorts?"

"I'm not sure, but I don't think so. When he comes, if he comes, you'll have no warning. I can't imagine who's commanding that mess out at sea. Things would certainly be different if I were planning the operation."

"Then I'm grateful you aren't planning it. We'll have no trouble killing you before a beach assault can reach you. But I'm not really interested in killing you. You've suffered quite enough to bring Mr. Duggan to my little paradise. The two young men accompanying me will be with you all the time now. If something happens, they will bring you to me. You're my shield, you see. Con Duggan will not fire on you."

"Yes, he will. He'll never let you off this island."

"Well said. I admire that about you. Con Duggan's people all react that way. He's only one man, you know. He'll come here, I'll kill him, and I'll get away. I always do."

"So far."

"Yes. Well, have you had a heart-to-heart with your father?"

"Briefly. He told me his protégé would save us, an Army general by the name of Cassidy."

"Ah, that must be the august mover and shaker, who's determined to make a name for himself. We—I—shall try desperately to stifle my fear of the man. Nothing else came from the conversation?"

"I have little to say to the senator."

"But he's your father, my dear."

"An unlucky biological accident. He's my father, and you are my rapist. I see only a slight difference between the two of you."

"Good! Then I've achieved my psychological goals far beyond my highest hopes. Now, one more task, and I shall be satisfied."

"You'll never kill him."

"Perhaps not, but I shall try." Without saying anything else, he left her alone with the two new guards.

Outwardly, Maggie remained calm, but inside, her heart raced, and her psyche struggled to survive. Whatever happened to her, she was determined to return the same old Maggie to her lover. She feared for his life, but not her own. Life and Con were inseparable to her, and one without the other was unthinkable. If Con went down in all this, she had resolved to kill Peter Coy Booker herself.

In the next cottage, her father was wide awake, staring out toward the sea and back into his own soul. It was a dark and difficult passage for him, but there was more to him than hedonism and a lust for power. He was also a father, and it was that aspect of his life he was trying to understand. The bimbo was drugged out and asleep, and as far as he could tell, nobody was watching him at all. The ultimate sign of disrespect from his captors. They saw the senator as a non-person.

The scientists on the naval base awakened abruptly when a black-painted C-130 slipped out of the darkness and landed on their secret turf, particularly since the plane used most of the runway and some of the adjacent gardens just to get it stopped. Their first reaction was surprise; their second was righteous indignation.

The base commander, a physicist by profession, stood below the nose of the C-130, shouting up to the cockpit even as it swung around and retraced its destructive path across his garden to point itself down the runway before shutting down its engines.

"Who the hell are you people, and what are you doing here? Do you people have any idea what's *on* this island?"

A tall, gray-haired man exited the loading ramp as it went down. He was dressed completely in black, his face blackened by charcoal, his visage made more fierce by his weaponry and his plane's sudden appearance out of the sky.

"Nope, what *do* you have here?" Con Duggan asked as if he had a real interest in whatever it was.

"Why, I can't tell you that!"

"Didn't think so, and we aren't going to snoop. We need your facility for a rescue mission. We've overridden your communications systems for the time being. Sorry about the flowers. There's plenty of goodies aboard this aircraft, so ask the loadmaster, the guy in the football jersey, for whatever you might want. Sorry about this. We'll see to our business and be outta here as soon as we can. By the way, what *do* you do here?"

"You'd never believe it."

"Try me."

"UFOs. We study UFOs."

Con Duggan stared at the scientist, but the man's face didn't change. It was, he thought, the most sincere face he'd ever seen.

"UFOs?" Con still couldn't quite believe it.

"Correct."

"Here?"

"Yes, here." Con wanted to ask if they *had* a UFO, but he didn't.

"We'll do our business and be gone. I can only tell you this is important."

" 'Kay, I can see that. But don't touch anything you don't recognize, all right? Very important!"

"Right. There's some good Scotch on the plane. Help yourself."

"Thanks, perhaps we will."

"I don't see anybody else."

"There are four of us here. We haven't been off this island since 1990. We all have one more year to go on our contract. Then, if we wish, we can sign on for five more years."

"I see. Well, no, I don't see. But just out of curiosity, will you elect to stay here?"

"Of course. We can't just *leave* them."

"Right. That would be bad. Well, like I said, help yourself to whatever we have. I mean it—if you see anything by the way of supplies you need, consider it our rent for using this place."

"Fair enough. Just remember, don't touch anything you don't recognize."

Nobody seemed surprised when Con told them not to touch the aliens. They went about their preparations, and at 0330, they lifted off in the *Whisper* and headed for Predator Bay, 177 miles distant. Flying at nearly wavetop height, nobody said much during the flight. What more could be said? They were flying off an island that might be a death trap, and they were going to kill a man they'd already killed once. What, really, was there to say?

As planned, the *Whisper* approached the island from the cliff side, all electronic sensors activated, blanketing the island. The night was very dark, with an occasional break of moonlight through the clouds. The temperature was mild, the wind nonexistent.

"*Whisper*, we have a cigarette-type boat tied up in an alcove. Shows crew and readiness."

"Acknowledged, 21A. Mark for later target. The getaway boat. O boy!"

The *Whisper* slipped up from the sea hopped over the clifftop, and then immediately swept down into one of the deep jungle "sockets" of the skull-shaped island's face.

"Two towers on right. Firing now."

Two "fire and forget" missiles zipped away from the *Whisper* and exploded against the tower bases. Gunfire arced into the air, shooting at the spot from which the missiles had been fired. The *Whisper* was long gone, and its mini-guns shot up the countryside with .25mm fire at a cyclic rate so fast the sound it made was like that of sheets tearing. In seconds, the *Whisper* had traversed the width of the island, and the mini-guns raked the northern beach tower, silencing it before it could even respond. The *Whisper* settled gently on the beach, and in seconds its pitifully small four-man assault team transformed Predator Bay into a war zone from hell.

The *Whisper* lifted off and began to hit targets all over the island, guided by the 21A–C-130 back at Chrystal Island. It had remained on the ground for this mission because the risk of takeoff from the island Con had dubbed "Alien Isle" was deemed too high to be attempted more than once.

At the first sound of gunfire, two things happened with the defenders. A large contingent of heavily armed men went into action, and Maggie was immediately taken to the bunker-like center of the Booker's house, his private sanctum.

"Well, Miss Stewart, I think this time it *is* Con Duggan. Leave it to him to figure a way to get a chopper right on the beach in the dark. It's a shame to kill him—almost. As you can see, we're well defended here, and if all goes badly, I shall just disappear down these stairs, with you in tow, of course, and pop up on the west beach below the cliffs. If Duggan survives, that is."

"General, we have activity on the island. Sir, the cap'n wants to see you," the messenger said.

"Oh, does he? Well, tell him I'll be along shortly, as soon as I finish this briefing."

"Sir, he said to tell you there seems to be an assault taking place on the island. From the volume of fire, he can't even hazard a guess who might be doing it."

General Cassidy bolted out of the mess hall and raced to the captain's side at the periscope.

"Let me look!"

"I think you're too late, General." The captain of the *Sea Dragon* didn't seem surprised.

Penelope James tripped in the soft island sand, then was pushed to the ground from behind by Con Duggan.

"Stay down! The chopper might draw fire when it leaves." A stream of red tracers flew overhead in answer to Con's thought.

"Get that tower!" Con yelled. Some of the bullets hitting the beach were striking the sand from above. A torrent of small-arms fire came from the house and surrounding buildings in the compound.

Even as Penelope prepared the SIKIM-1000 for Steven Dye, as she slapped on the box-like magazine of .40 caliber explosive shells, she noted how different, how much finer and softer to the touch, this Caribbean sand was compared to that of English beaches. She had no way to know the sand fronting the house had been imported, four tons of it, from the shores of South Africa at considerable cost.

She tapped Steven on the head to signal that the SIKIM was ready, and he immediately shredded the tower nearest the road, the roar of the weapon shockingly loud and close, jarring her into the harsh reality of where she was, why they were there, and that she might very easily get killed on this very spot.

The fire from above them stopped. Con and Michael were up and running toward the house, Con's German-made submachine gun barking loudly in contrast to the sharp snapping sound of Michael's M-16. Both men also carried two pistols, extra cartridges for their weapons, two knives, and four stun grenades.

Steven Dye jumped up, heading for the disabled tower. For a moment, Penelope James stood there, her slim, heavily loaded body shaking for no reason.

"The tower! Go to the tower!" Con's voice came from in front of her, his guns flashing as he threw himself headfirst through the blasted-open front door, followed at once by Michael.

Quickly, she joined Steven on the tower platform and began the process of unburdening herself of the many ammunition belts and specialized barrels necessary to "serve the Suckem" as she called her function when in action. She laid the barrels out, arranged the long belt feeds for the .50 caliber, and set out the EDRs, energy depletion rounds, as well, though they were not likely to be needed. Steven would primarily use the three regular calibers and explosive rounds. Much of the shooting from the tower would be pure sniping. Quiet shooting, he called it.

The sophisticated scope was powered up and functioning,

and he began to find targets in the dark. All the time, the steel tower itself took fire.

Explosions rocked the high ridge above them as Ivan Tescher and the *Whisper* began to work over all possible targets. Penelope watched in fascination as explosions lit up the dark "eye socket" area while the *Whisper* itself remained nearly invisible. Within twenty minutes, gunfire from the surrounding jungle ceased, and a string of ten to fifteen men filed out onto the beach, hands high over their heads.

"Do you see them, Penelope?" the *Whisper's* pilot radioed.

"Roger, *Whisper*. What now?"

"Go down to the beach and disarm them."

"Me? Alone?"

"We can't leave them out there, Penelope. Go check them out."

A bullet hit the tower and ricocheted inside the round-walled, defensive weapons station. The walls were all metal, and she could hear it clang around and finally stop at her feet. She reached out her hand to touch it, but pulled back. Then she climbed down the stairs and started across the beach, moving in crisscross little runs of 15 to 20 feet. She carried her custom-made, .12-gauge street-sweeper shotgun, and a Glock .9mm pistol was strapped to her waist.

"Sit down, all of you! Put your hands on your heads!" There was a distinct air of authority in her British voice that was in stark contrast to her sleek body and slight build. There were fifteen macho mercenaries who didn't look so cocky any longer. Most of them obeyed her, some did not.

"Don't you understand? Sit down! I have to make sure you have no weapons."

"Ah, but pretty girl, with such as you, we no need weapons, yes? I no theenk so. We just take ours, okay? We think beeg army is here, but is just this little fuckable girl with funny voice.'

Penelope raised the shotgun level and pointed it at the speaker. "Do as I say, and you won't be hurt. We don't want you. We want the Yankee woman. We don't want to kill you."

"Ah. You no shoot beeg gun, yes? We not know you only girl and . . ."

Penelope pulled the trigger, and the man flew backward as if jerked by some powerful force. She leveled the gun again and shot the next two who were still standing. Now all of them were down.

"Stand up!" She screamed at them, shaking with rage and fear. . . . Off behind her, Steven's .30 caliber cracked once, and someone off to her right screamed, thrashed around in the bushes near the beach, and stumbled out of cover and fell onto the beach, arms and legs spread wide, eyes open, a .45 still clutched in his hand.

Mentally, she racked up points for Steven. She would find a suitable way to pay him back later.

The shock of seeing three men nearly cut in half, and the long, deadly shot from the tower killing a man in the darkened jungle, was enough. They stood up.

"Strip! Take off your bloody clothes! I'm plenty brassed off, I am, and I'll not tolerate any more delay!"

In very little time the remaining dozen men were standing naked on the beach before her as the clouds parted and flooded the area with moonlight. Now she herself felt vulnerable.

"All of you, hit it! Get into the water! Swim for it!"

"Señora, where should we swim *to*?"

"I don't care. Haiti is fairly close, a few hundred miles. I don't care. I must get to the house! Go! Swim!" She fired the shotgun again very near the huddled group and peppered them with loose sand kicked up by the blast of the heavy .12-gauge slug. Without more prompting, they ran to, and then into, the warm waters of the Caribbean. For an instant, she admired their nakedness; they all seemed to be very fit. She pushed the neck switch at her throat and spoke directly to 21A, 177 miles away.

"This is Penelope. Beach is cleared. I'm on my way to the house as planned. Con and Michael are inside, I hope. Steven contained all periphery fire from east tower at beach road. Penelope out."

"Received, Miss James. 21A out."

As she moved off slowly toward the house in a semi-crouch, the sound of men splashing as they swam mingled with the normal surf sounds and then disappeared. As she drew even with the boat dock, a gun roared and flashed from aboard the *Assassin,* anchored there without lights. She felt an impact in her shoulder and was knocked violently to the ground. She'd been hit. White lights flashed behind her eyes, then a rush of pain swept over her, and she threw up onto the sand, her body shaking, the rusty smell of fresh blood, her own blood, assailing her nostrils.

"Steven Yank, I'm hit! From the boat! Get the boat!" She lay on the sand for what seemed an eternity, and then another shot from the boat whistled over her head, very near her face.

"Steven, get the dirty bast—"

From the tower came a bright blue, unearthly glow, followed by a streak of light toward the boat. Steven's TAD rounds, the thermal accelerating device, slammed its shaped charge into the boat's cabin and turned it immediately into a very expensive mass of burning wood. The fire raged furiously from one end of the craft to the other, lighting the area for a hundred yards all around.

Penelope passed out just as Steven reached her side and began to cut away her combat pack, which had blown apart when the bullet hit it on the way to her shoulder. At least the light from the fire was good enough for him to see what he was doing.

"Cover me, Ivan, till I zip up our little girl down here." Instantly, he felt, though he didn't see, the *Whisper* overhead. He bent to look at her shoulder, cutting away at the uniform material until her left arm was bare.

"It's clean, sweetie. Went right through," Steven told her.

She seemed alert again and heartened by his presence. "Well, bind it up then, and let's get on with this."

"It's going to hurt, but you'll live."

"Goody. Now hurry." As usual, Steven did what she told him when she told him to do it. He made no attempt to stop her or suggest her evacuation. In minutes, looking barbaric with only one sleeve surviving on her uniform top and a bloody bandage tightly wrapped around her upper shoulder and arm, she continued on to the house without so much as saying thanks.

Steven returned to the SIKIM-1000 system in the tower and began a sweep of the area, shooting at everything within range of his gun. Out to sea, he could clearly see the running lights of a submarine, as if advertising its presence would reassert calm on the island.

The island was quieter now, with only scattered gunfire. Now the work would get personal—and messy. Steven kept the SIKIM-1000 working, reducing the odds against the team with each shot. Behind him, the boat and sails that he had gone to so much trouble to find burned down to the waterline and hissed out. Now it was up to Con and Michael, accmpanied by the bleeding but still functioning British expeditionary force. Penelope, he knew, would be okay.

13

Assault on the Compound
4:50 A.M. January 5, 1994

Con glanced at his watch. Almost 0500. They had been on the island for just a little over forty-five minutes. Too slow. They were moving too slowly. He rested his back against a wall in a darkened, spoke-like hallway he'd reached after passing through the outer core of rooms unscathed. Fingers of hallway stretched toward the center of the compound, some roofed, others open to the sky. A conversation piece of sophisticated architecture in more passive times, it was a deadly series of lead-ins, alternately open or shut, some dark, some brightly lit, some with flashing strobes to confuse the intruder. The halls, each about fifty or sixty feet long, had cameras and speakers randomly placed and doors at varying locations, some leading to other passageways, some to rooms occupied by armed men or dogs. Rock and roll music blared from the speakers. It was the scariest place Booker could imagine, and he had built it to suit his imagination.

The sound harrassment was quickly taken care of by simply shooting out the speakers. The lighting was more deeply protected.

"Con, where are you?" Michael's voice in his earphones.

"In a kind of hallway, center house."

"Me too. A little to your left. Probably one hall separates us. You got doors in there?"

"One door at the end."

"I got four. Can you get over here?"

"Never mind, Con. I see him." Penelope's voice, strained and high.

"Do you see her, Michael?"

"She's with me, Con. Jesus, what happened to you?"

"What! What!" Con feared his operation was going to fail, fought back the thought, and watched as the door at the end of the hall slid open, left to right, into the wall. The opening seemed to beckon to him.

"I've been bloody shot, that's fucking wot! Hell of a place to bring a young popsie like me!" She fell against Michael and had a short, hard cry, and then sat up, looking strong and determined. "I'm all right, Con. We've got to reach Maggie."

"Concur, Penelope. Michael, look after that girl."

"I can look after myself!" she protested.

The open door at the end of Con's hallway was suddenly filled of men bearing weapons, and he brought the ugly little German automatic up and hosed them down. The corridor light went off.

"Nice going, Mr. Duggan. Now what?" Booker's voice, from somewhere, from everywhere, from nowhere. Con swept the hallway again. Three men were down and there was a bullet tear at the elbow of Con's shirt, the closest he'd come to being hit so far. He moved ahead, a man compelled, blood rising in his throat.

"Con, look out!" Maggie's voice! He stopped, realized Booker's game, and moved on around the corner. It was a dummy wall, and he was joined immediately by his teammates.

"A sick man, that one," Michael said unecessarily.

"Which way, Michael?"

"You lead, Con. You know me. I'm a producer, not a director." The phony hallway led on and extended into a kind of recreation room with pinball machines, a piano, and scattered pieces of furniture in a space that looked to be at least forty feet across.

"A lot of this is just whistles and bells," Con told them. "Try to ignore the lights and sounds. We'll have to meet

and defeat the guards. When they're all down, Booker
will make *his* move to kill us. Until then, don't worry
about Maggie. Don't listen if you hear her voice, and don't
respond to sounds or light, because right in the middle of
it are some bad guys with guns. Nothing super, just bad
guys."

As Con Duggan led the team away from the dummy
hallways and into the room, they came under heavy fire
and found themselves involved in close combat. Five nearly
naked men rushed them, backed up by two men with pistols
firing from behind the piano and a pinball machine.

One of the backup shooters didn't shoot very straight and
hit the man closest to Con in the back instead, killing him. He
fell into, and out of, Con's hands. He seemed to be covered
in an oil of some kind. Each of the attackers carried only a
knife and wore a simple braided belt at the waist, similar to
the braid of his hair. They appeared to be Indians, possibly
from South America.

"Oooo-uuuck! Look at the dick on that one," Penelope,
ever observant, said just as an assailant caught her around
the throat and hurled her to the floor before she could bring
the shotgun to bear. She cried out in pain, and Michael
leaped onto the man's back, but found no hold. He stood
back finally and put the barrel of his 9mm Glock flush on
the man's head and pulled the trigger, knocking the man
violently off Penelope.

She groaned in pain, her face splattered with blood and
oil from her now-dead attacker.

"Jesus, Michael. Jesus H. Christ."

"Yes, I know. Hang on, girl. It's worse than I'd expected
and planned for. Stay with me. I shouldn't have allowed you
to participate in the . . ."

Her shouted warning was followed by six shotgun blasts
so close together they were indistinguishable from one
another. The remaining "naked men with knives and salad
oil on," as Penelope would always refer to them, took four
of the rounds, while the pinball machine and the pistolero
behind it exploded in fragments of glass, steel balls, lights,
mirrors, and flesh from the final two shots.

The man behind the piano was firing steadily at Con Duggan, who was crouched behind a large sofa, trying to get a shot off, but failing to get clear enough to respond.

Penelope ran toward him, the shotgun roaring, but doing little more than scaring him off Con while she chewed a twenty-thousand-dollar piano into little bits of wood and ivory. Con jumped up, unnoticed, and shot the distracted man twice in the chest.

The shotgun had started a fire in the pinball machine, which electronically kept running up points on the flashing but glassless scoreboard. Untended, the fire threatened to burn the house down. The team halted for a moment to put out the flames, pounding them down with curtains torn from the shattered windows. The fire out, somewhere under the blackened curtains, the machine kept running up the score.

"Oh, bloody hell," said Penelope before shooting the machine into a twelve-gauge silence.

Fifty yards away, Maggie's father, the patriotic, brave United States Senator, remained in his quarters, unguarded. His "roommate" had long since disappeared without him, her saucy ass the last thing he saw going out the door only an instant after the *Whisper* began to shoot up the ridge installations. Gunfire seemed to come from all around him, and he sat immobile on the bed, afraid to do anything.

The door finally popped open, and a gore- and smoke-covered trio stood in his doorway.

"Hello, Senator, where's Maggie?" Con Duggan stepped forward followed by Michael.

Penelope James split off and moved down the hallway, kicking in doors as she went.

"Who are you? How did you get here?"

"Where's Maggie?"

The senator finally reacted and recognized whom he was speaking to. "Con? Con Duggan."

"Right. Where's Maggie?" Con seemed ready to strike the older man, and the senator cringed backward, his knees striking the edge of the bed and plopping him onto it with little decorum. He was drunk as well, wearing only shorts, and barefoot. He looked sunburned.

"Senator, my name is Michael. Do you remember me from the party?"

"A party? Oh, New Year's Eve." Had it been that short a time?

"Please, sir, we must find your daughter. Every second counts."

"I must be told what has happened here. I must . . ."

"Penelope!"

"Yes, Con!" He heard the girl respond from somewhere outside, heard the SIKIM-1000 go off, probably in .40 caliber mode, then heard an explosion that seemed right outside the compound. Steven was destroying the cars and trucks trying to reach the beach road. None would.

"Con, you need me?" Penelope asked when it was quieter.

"Yes, take the senator back to Steven. Tell Steven to keep him up there, out of the way. Tell Steven to shoot him if he does anything to hinder our operation."

"What—why, you can't do that, I'm a . . ."

Penelope stepped forward and stuck her shotgun into the senator's paunch. "Maggie's just like a mother to me. If you want to be treated like my grandfather, do as Mr. Duggan says, and come with me."

The senator looked at Maggie's "daughter," bloody, dirty, wearing a soiled bandage that still leaked fresh blood down her forearm. She looked very pale and gaunt and quite a bit crazy as well. A bit of someone's brain tissue was stuck to the fabric of her assault uniform above the breast, stark against the black fabric.

"Well, Senator?" Penelope's patience was wearing thin.

Now the senator docilely followed her out the door, stopping to inform Con and Michael that his daughter's quarters were right next to his.

"She's not there, Con, I checked," Penelope said.

"She's with Booker, Mr. Duggan. You're going to get her killed!" the Senator wailed.

Con only grimaced and stepped aside for Penelope and

Maggie's father to leave the room and head for Steven's position in the beach tower.

"Makes you wonder about genetics, doesn't it, Con?" Michael said.

Con, however, was already out the door.

The senator stumbled along behind the sure-footed Penelope, the dawn fading in and pushing the night away.

In an hour, it would be full daylight. The Confirmed Kill Team preferred to hunt in the dark. It evened the terrible odds against them.

"Hello, Steven Dye. The government part of the mission is a success—got us a senator," Penelope announced as she entered the damaged tower.

Steven crushed her to him, and she moaned in pain and once again began to bleed from the shoulder. Her skin was the color of a vampire, ghostlike and unnatural.

Bullets rattled off the outside wall, and the senator screamed in alarm, "They're shooting at us!"

"Hey, Steven Dye, how's about changing the bloody bandage for a bloody clean one?" Even shot up, Penelope kept the spark that made her nearly indestructible.

"I said, they're shooting at us!" The senator's voice was higher than natural, his eyes wide saucers of open fear.

"Really? Why don't you shoot back?" Steven changed the bandage, then arranged the senator in what he thought might be a safe place down the tower steps.

"21A, Delta air team en route. Twenty, repeat, twenty minutes till drop."

All four members of the team responded affirmatively to the message, and Con muttered disgustedly. "Jesus Christ, the cavalry." That summation seemed to fit this bit of information best. In spite of his sarcasm, though, he was also genuinely concerned. He thought the airdropped units would be in very serious trouble very quickly.

General Cassidy, the Delta Force leader, had all but cancelled the carefully wrought plans that had brought him to the submarine off the beaches of Predator Bay. He finally knew who was on the island, though he didn't know, and couldn't imagine, how this band of freelancers had found the place. He had ignored the not-too-subtle hints from his Washington connections that Duggan's efforts might bear fruit now. He'd called in the airdrop an hour early and was trying to launch his SEAL force from the submarine. There was a gang fight of considerable size on the island, and his senator was right in the middle of it. The senator's survival and appreciation for his rescue had been General Cassidy's driving force. Now he wanted in on the fight at any level.

"I have come for the senator." Steven Dye spun away from the SIKIM scope, startled by the calmness of the voice that penetrated the pockets of sporadic gunfire as he watched the Delta Force airdrop scatter itself across the ridge and down into the deep jungle "eye" sockets.

As the light of the approaching dawn cleared away some of the haze of battle, Steven found himself confronted by a large Oriental man wearing, not holding, a pistol. He knew instantly who it was.

"You're Chin?"

"I am. How do you know of me?"

"SCAR."

"I know no one called Scar."

"No, it's a machine. Not a human, a machine."

"I am relieved to know that. Senator, I must take you to your daughter. She and Booker will soon be forced to retreat to a preassigned means of escape. I must take you with me."

The senator stood up, trying to act dignified, but he was frightened and unsure of himself and couldn't conceal it. He collapsed back to the tower deck. "I'm not going anywhere," he moaned.

"Oh, but you must. You must atone for your shameful behavior. A father who allows his child to be raped and fails to respond has much to answer for. Centuries ago in the Orient, girl babies were routinely abandoned at birth. You have waited until now to desert your girl baby. Booker does not know I am doing this—he has no interest in you—but I will take you to her. You must erase her shame."

"Did you hear me? I'm not going with you. These men will find my daughter." Now the senator was getting agitated.

"Yes, they will. They may even save her from death. But if she lives, she must live with your disgrace. I know about such things—I have six daughters. You must make this right."

Steven Dye measured the distance between the two men and the differences between him and Chin. Both of them were skilled in the martial arts. Chin was bigger and stronger, and Steven Dye had gone through both previous missions without a personal confrontation. He and the SIKIM-1000 had done their jobs. Technically, he was an unqualified success as the team's ace shooter. This time, however, he was the man on the spot, whether he liked it or not.

"The senator stays," Steven said and stepped away from the SIKIM-1000, its lethal look diminished when he was not manning the weapon.

"You are a foolish young man. I do not want to kill you, or I would have shot you in the back, even while the senator watched without crying out a warning."

"The senator stays." Steven's voice was firm and strong.

Chin regarded Steven Dye with a look that evolved from perplexed anger through wry amusement to settle on hard, cold-eyed preparation.

"You are a fool, boy," Chin said, and then the husky Oriental wasn't standing in the doorway any longer. He had launched himself into the air, one leg cocked, the toe of the other foot pointed at Steven's neck. Steven reacted almost as quickly, parred the kick, and took only a glancing blow to the cheek, but that was still strong enough to knock him down.

Steven bounced to his feet and slashed out at Chin in moves from a long-forgotten *Shudokan Kata,* ten years of daily training put to the fatal test for the first time.

His fists flew at the larger man and struck home, followed by two straight throat kicks and a multiple four-move strike of swishing, swapping side kicks. With each punch and kick, explosive sounds erupted from the two men, who were

silently regarding each other with newfound respect. Blood
trickled from the corner of Steven's mouth, and blood ran
in a steady stream from a cut above his eye, and he kept
wiping at it with the back of his hand like a prizefighter.
His left wrist, after blocking a vicious kick aimed at his
head, was numb, and if not broken, at least badly sprained
or the nerves damaged. As he surveyed Chin, he could see
no outward sign of injury.

"Give up?" asked Steven, a crooked smile on his bloodied
face. In answer, Chin rushed forward, leading with kicks and
following up with fists. It was the only move Chin made
that the less experienced, both emotionally and physically,
younger man could counter with deadly effect. His *sensai*,
believing Steven to be a gifted student, had taught him a
little-used "fold-out" attack that functioned like a Swiss
Army knife suddenly opened with all its utensils ready for
use. It could only be attempted once, because if it failed,
you finished in an erect position, and were for all intents
and purposes, weaponless.

Steven absorbed all the blows of Chin's attack, ignoring
with mystic determination the pain shooting through his
chest and arms. He turned away, his back to his opponent,
then "unfolded" with a lightning-fast rear throat kick,
followed by sweeping, cutting attacks with the backs of
his hands, and two thunderous heart kicks. His body then
recovered, and he stood completely exposed, his hands in
only a casual defensive posture. Steven looked at Chin,
standing in front of him, the man's face contorted with
pain and disbelief. Chin made an ineffectual gesture and
then toppled over at Steven's feet, face first. He didn't
move. Silence fell in the tower, a blanket over the sounds
of combat now limited to Steven's heavy, tired breathing.

"Is he out?" The senator moved to the center of the
tower and bent over a little, looking down at the massive,
seemingly invincible martial artist, Booker's oldest and most
trusted associate.

"No, he's not out, he's dead. I exploded his heart and
severed his windpipe." Steven looked up at the senator
and tried to staunch the flow of blood from the cut above

his eyebrow. At that moment, Penelope burst back into the tower.

"The house is cleared, and Booker's off through the woods with Maggie! Con's hunting him, and Michael's heading for the cigarette boat. We're to pack up and follow because Booker has a dozen men left. The paratroops are on the way, SEAL units are paddling ashore, and we . . . Steven, whatever did you do to your face?"

With that, Steven Dye passed out on top of his assailant.

"It will leave a lovely, sexy scar. Makes me wet just thinking about it. One day you can scar-fuck me." Penelope delivered her litany in a singsong voice designed to divert her patient from what she was doing.

Steven, lost in the warmth of her ministrations, dazedly tried to imagine a scar-fuck. Let me see. She lays down, and I put my eye in her . . . no, on her . . . or . . .

"What are you going to do with me?" Now that Steven was injured, the senator looked to Penelope for information and instructions.

"Nothing, Senator. Con Duggan told me to pick up Steven and our gear and get to the coast through the jungle. There's a nice road hidden under the trees. I expect he'll want you to be there to meet the chaps rowing ashore in their little yellow rubber boats. The bloody American Navy. They'll liberate you. We have to get to Maggie and kill Booker. You'd best make sure the general knows we can't tell the goodies from the baddies without a flam'n scorecard. A real killing zone in there. You best keep your stuffy self out of the jungle. C'mon, honey Yank, you look just fine. Here, drink this."

"What is it?" Steven was skeptical when it came to consuming unidentified liquids proffered by his British paramour.

"Don't know. Con said if you were still alive, I was to give it to you, and he made me promise: no sex! I'm bloody horny!"

"Mostly you're bloody."

"Yes, aren't we both now? Drink your joy juice. We have to hurry."

"You can't leave me here." There was an edge of hysteria in the senator's voice.

"Sure I can, Senator, and I'm going to." Penelope stowed all the assorted pieces of the SIKIM into their gear bags and plopped the lot out the window. A dark shape rose up, crossed the open space, and moved almost soundlessly away. Full dawn was near. The *Whisper* disappeared from sight over the ridge.

"What was that?" Everything was disconcerting to the senator now.

"That was the *Whisper*, our helicopter. A lovely machine. At a certain speed, there is a positively lovely, sexy place to sit in it. But that's girl stuff, isn't it?" She gave the senator a broad, slow wink.

Penelope pulled Steven to his feet, but he was still wobbly from combat, pain, and blood loss.

"Drink your stuff!" she ordered.

He drank it, choked a bit, and smiled. She swung two canvas and Velcro bandoliers of .12 gauge shotgun shells over her shoulders, and for an instant looked like one of Pancho Villa's dusky bandit maidens. Love for her swept over Steven like a soft warm blanket. Actually, it was the potion of booze and uppers he'd just tossed down. Joy juice, indeed. Pulled behind the still-sexy, albeit tattered, Miss James, Steven left the senator alone in the tower, and went with her to the front of the house. Out of sight, they exited into the jungle. As they did so, the first rubber boats hit the shore and the Delta Force sea contingent arrived with virtually no opposition.

14

Michael had been in the jungle before. But Predator Bay, except where civilization had been imposed on its verdant hills, remained much as it had been since it first emerged from the sea over two hundred years before the Constitution of the United States had been penned.

Vietnam had had its mountains, its paddies, and its cities, but to Michael, its most terrible battle zone had always been the jungle. This island was alive with birds, loud, raucus birds that seemed to drown out even the sound of gunfire.

Only a couple hundred yards ahead, Booker moved toward the cliff coast. Occasionally Maggie called out, begging Con and his team to stay back, that Booker would kill them all.

But they moved on, into the deep jungle sockets, where every bush had a possible gun. Delta Force had flown over, dropped its people, and flown off. As far as Michael could tell, most of them were dead or down. As a fighting force, they had been reduced to hiding. The jungle was alive with doped-up natives from someplace else, all carrying automatic weapons. He had no way of knowing, but the drop and the resulting jungle firefight had killed 38 of the 51 invading troops. On the other hand, confirmed kills littered the beach compound, and now nobody on the southern half of the island was resisting. But here, in the "eyes" of the jungle, death seemed to lurk everywhere.

131

Michael Barns was afraid. It had been a while since he'd experienced that sensation, but now he was scared. He'd come across a beheaded man wearing a jumpsuit but carrying NBC identification papers. Jesus, film at eleven. General Cassidy had badly misjudged Mr. Peter Coy Booker. Hopefully, the senator, safe and sound at the beach, was reward enough for an anxious government, casualties be damned.

The sharp cough of an Uzi erupted nearby, sending lead zipping overhead and pinning him to the ground.

"*Whisper!*" Michael hissed into his radio.

'Roger, this is *Whisper*."

"Can you clear any of this out? Booker's just strolling through like a guy on the way to the store."

"His people, Michael."

"Goddamnit, you crazy Russian, I know they're his people! Can you kill them?"

"Yes and no."

"What's the no part?"

"Con Duggan. He said the *Whisper* is the only tool we have to counter Delta. Yes, I can get down in there, but I'm no more invisible now than a fucking jungle parrot."

"Understood. Negative on the help, *Whisper*, but stay around that speedboat. Blow it out of the water if you have to. If possible, keep them off the boat till we get there."

"Roger, but you understand, they're walking and you're crawling."

Shadows flitted everywhere, and the darkness of the green foliage was splashed with astonishingly beautiful flowers and occasional variegated leaves. Paradise. To die for, as Penelope would say. Off to his left, Michael heard the .12 gauge go off, three distinct, thumping roars, a sound different from any other weapon on the island. Bless her. This child/woman had come to the team like a miracle, by "bus," as she laughingly referred to her arrival. Gone a bit crazy since, perhaps, but who hadn't?

A chunk of lead thunked into the soft, dark earth near him, burrowed up between his spread legs, and stopped just short of causing some serious damage to a very sensitive area.

Somewhere out front, a man laughed, a woman screamed, then silence. Somebody very close was shooting at him, but who and where?

A string of bullets chopped through some giant palmetto leaves; one round tore through his shoe, exited between two toes, and took one toe off on its journey. He let out a scream and rolled behind a huge dead tree covered with moss. He heard somebody rushing his way, so he held the twin .9mm Glocks pointed directly into the green screen surrounding his position. Penelope popped through and landed very hard, sitting up next to him, aiming her shotgun ahead and high into the trees. She fired four rounds, was empty, and while reloading the circular drum magazine from one of her bandoliers, she eyed his foot.

"Oops! Take off your shoe. I'll tape it up. I'm turning into a bloody wonderful Penelope Nightingale. Me, you, Steven Yank." It was her first acknowledgement of Michael's presence.

"Steven is hit?" he asked.

"Not by bullets. He and an Oriental, a very large Oriental, had a get-together. The Oriental lost, and now he's dead, but Steven's beat up a bit. His hand's broken, I think, and he lost some blood. He'll have a terrific scar, though! Very Bondish."

A dark form rushed their position, and without wasted effort, Penelope dispatched the man by tearing the jungle to bits with her shotgun. Task completed, she turned back to speak. "I heard Maggie! She cries out once in a while and tells us to go back."

"Where are Steven and Con now?" Michael wasn't sure she'd know, but he was desperate for all the information he could get.

"Con's moving toward the boat, trying to avoid contact. Steven's resting. He can't hold a weapon properly, so I left him with half a dozen grenades. He's safe."

When she finished, Penelope looked down at Michael's foot again. He was toying with his boot and not moving it much. "Not like that. Pull the boot off." With that, she jerked the boot from his foot. Clearly, the end of his sock was shot off. Clearer still, he had no little toe on his right foot. Penelope looked at the foot, turned the boot upside down, and shook it. Out rolled the toe. She caught it deftly in her free hand and pulled a plastic zip-lock–type bag with pot in it out of her pocket. She dumped the pot and dropped the toe in the bag, then poured a cup or so of liquid into it from a penis-shaped flask.

"Naughty, huh? Vibrators, too. A girl never knows. This is straight rum. It'll pickle your little piggie. I think you ought to keep it, don't you? Wear it on a chain or something." Penelope sealed the bag and handed it to him. It was then he noticed the tears streaming down her powder-blackened face.

"Not much more, Penelope." He reached out to her, but she pulled back.

"Oh, yes, there's a lot more. I keep killing them, but then I bandage someone. There's more, Michael. Don't you understand? We like it. We, all of us on the team, we love this!"

The bullets from above started again, and Penelope watched them walk their way between them. She raised her hands, indicating two, and pointed up. With a few more hand motions, he got the idea. She pulled his other boot off and threw it into the jungle.

"Better without shoes," she told him.

Michael glanced down, and she was barefoot too, her feet impossibly slim and feminine, bright red toenails poking into the dirt. She motioned once more and crawled away into the jungle. He followed, angling about twenty yards to her left. Suddenly it was very quiet. The two shooters, if Penelope was correct about the number, were very, very close to them in the stinking, dark jungle.

Even the birds had stopped squawking. Earthbound mammals and reptiles had ceased moving. Ahead of him, he heard soft thuds, evenly spaced, but he couldn't identify the sound. He pushed forward. It got louder. He stopped, every muscle straining to keep still, wanting to run for his life. *Thtup-thtup-thtup.* What kind of sound was that? He moved forward, and large droplets of blood, previously dropping on a hollow log, began to drop on his right arm. *Thup, thup, thup.* He rolled onto his back, pointed both 9mm's overhead, and began to fire. Thirty feet away, the shotgun roared out six times, and a body dropped like a sack of grain from a tall palm tree. Directly over Michael's head, a dead man hung bent forward, arms dangling loosely down, held by a leather belt to the tree. The hands relaxed their grasp, and Michael had to pivot on his throbbing right foot to get out of the way of the Uzi the man had been trying to kill him with.

When Penelope joined him, she redid the bandages on his foot, and he retaped her shoulder. She was very pale, nearly out on her feet.

"Soon, Michael. Just a little more." Now it was her turn to bolster his morale.

She helped him to his feet, and he let her lead her cat's way into a jungle she seemed born to.

General Cassidy stood on the beach looking very impressive in his black Delta Force uniform with its distinctive patches and gray accents. CNN already had personnel, cameras, and a satellite dish on shore and was broadcasting live and non-stop from the scene of the heaviest action. The on-camera reporter was clearly disappointed he'd missed the actual fighting, but he managed to keep up a meaningful-sounding narration as the cameras panned and repanned the area of the greatest carnage. From time to time a camera focused on Cassidy, and the general did his best not to let the television audience down.

Cassidy had lost all but three of his paratroopers in an ill-advised jump into hostile fire, yet now he was standing on a sunny beach littered with enemy bodies, with the United States Senator he had been sent to rescue standing next to him, speaking to the President of the United States via CNN, as well as the world. He, General Cassidy, had, by God, rescued the captive senator, and they both now stood among the vanquished dead. The general did the things that generals do, walking among his victorious assault troops who had expended two thousand small-arms rounds against an undefended beach. Now they claimed to have achieved a smashing victory over terrorism.

While the CNN cameras broadcast the devastation on the beach, the senator and the general walked toward the dock that had been the home of the *Assassin*. Only the rope used to tie her to the dock served as evidence she had ever been there.

"Well, Senator, were you ever worried?" General Cassidy asked with a forced tone of concern.

"About what?"

"Rescue—whether or not we'd execute a successful operation." From the jungle, a long string of gunfire, punctuated by low, muffled explosions, startled the general.

"My daughter is in there, someplace," the senator said.

"Don't worry, Senator. That's a very competent para unit I dropped in there."

"My guess is that most of them are dead."

"What! Why?"

"Do you see any of them? Are you in contact with them yet?"

"Not yet, but I sent a SEAL patrol in there as soon as we hit the beach."

More gunfire ripped across the gulley.

"Penelope." The senator said her name with no explanation.

"What?"

"Penelope, they call her. She has this monstrous shotgun. I recognize the sound."

"A woman? Up *there?*"

"She's a member of Con Duggan's team. They rescued me, General, but I know you're aware of that. For now, I won't bring it up, but I recommend strongly you keep your men out of that hellhole."

"You mean Duggan's *team* is up there?"

"Of course. He's my daughter's life partner. You should have anticipated it."

"But the President gave him a direct order to stay out of this."

"Con Duggan breaks ranks sometimes. You might try to remember that I am alive and able to continue to support you through future appropriations thanks to him. Stand aside now, Cassidy, and let things flow."

"Damned if I will!"

"Suit yourself."

A heavily armed trooper from the SEAL unit brought the general a field radio. Cassidy listened, then handed it back to the trooper.

"Any message, sir?"

"No message. Wait! Tell them to break contact is all. We'll have to go around."

"General?" The senator was curious.

"Chopped my patrol down a bit. I've ordered them back to the beach. Senator, I think you'd best go out to the sub."

"Wrong, General. The photo opportunities are right here. Go get my daughter or Booker if you think you have to be involved. But be forewarned: If you fail, or if you screw up Con Duggan's operation, your whole fucking career is right down the toilet—and that's not a threat, it's a promise!"

Cassidy, without the slightest idea how to find the senator's daughter, just stood there on the beach looking into the rising sun.

The gunfire rose and fell in waves, then died to only single, sporadic shots. The island finally grew silent, and after a short time, the birds began to sing again.

And what was the status of the senator's daughter? asked CNN. Embarrassed, the general had no answer. People all over the world watched live on CNN as a two star general shrugged his shoulders and walked away. He realized he was in no position to get to her and so advised the President. He ordered his troops into the jungle and just six in rubber boats to scout the far cliffs. Knowing that Con Duggan and his people were on Predator Bay without authorization, General Cassidy was advised that as of this moment, Delta Force was to "await and conform to" Con Duggan's plans or instructions. The Confirmed Kill Team was officially authorized "to be afield at this time." That left the options open so the top brass in Washington could take whatever action the final outcome of Con's operation warranted: medals and adulation if it was successful, prison sentences and disgrace if it was not.

The search and rescue mission to find Maggie had finally narrowed itself in scope, proscribed by geography from utilizing any tactic except confrontation. The area available for maneuvering, for both kidnapper and rescuer, had shrunk to the point that all participants were now within one hundred yards of each other.

Penelope James sat with her slim back against a fallen tree, her feet in a cool stream rushing down the heights from above her. She could smell the ocean and knew she was very close to Maggie, separated, she was sure, by the green wall between her position and the rocky cliffs. Off to her left, a wide, well-used trail wound its way through the jungle and down to the narrow beach. Maggie was there, she was sure of it. But the water was cool on Penelope's feet, she was exhausted, and more than anything else, she was leaderless at the moment.

"21A, where is everybody?" she whispered into her radio.

"I'm right where you left me, babe," Steven Dye responded. The audio was very clear. The sophisticated communications system never ceased to amaze her.

"Good for you, Steven Yank. You rest."

"I'll be with you in five minutes, Penelope," Michael replied. "There doesn't seem to be any gunfire right now."

"Received, Michael. Five minutes."

"Con, where are you?" Penelope used her "help" tone of voice.

Silence. Nothing. Penelope watched the comforting water rush over her feet, her polished toenails bright crimson and clean, a small, sexy piece of her free of dirt and grime to anchor her sanity. She couldn't help it, she'd counted. She had personally killed twenty-nine men. Confirmed. She bit into a bitter-tasting chocolate bar she'd taken from the body of a dead paratrooper. It tasted lousy, but she needed the energy. She wondered if she should just toddle down to the base of the cliff and see Maggie. She closed her eyes—just for a minute. Sleep—just a little rest. Michael would wake her up. . . .

Michael, limping badly on his injured foot, came to the small stream and sat down next to the sleeping Penelope. He let her sleep, taking the time to minister to his four-toed foot, rebandaging it and cutting himself a twisted tree root to use as a make-do crutch. He too soaked his wounds, the water first rushing over Penelope's feet, then his. It was a beatific interlude in the midst of what seemed to be an unending horror.

21A had advised them they were at least quasi-legal now, and that gained them a measure of respectability if nothing else. The President had asked to be patched through to Michael. Instead of chewing him a new asshole, the President thanked the team for "disobeying" orders he knew they'd ignore in the first place. So all was reasonably well with the 21A world, except that Maggie was still a hundred yards away and, as reported by the *Whisper,* sitting on the long forward deck of the hopped-up cigarette boat.

Booker was there too, of course, as were two motorized rubber boats with SEALS aboard, one submarine, and CNN's media people who were panting in exhaustion but trying like hell to get some more blood for the late-morning news.

"*Whisper?*"

"Michael?"

"Yeah. What's it like down there?"

"About ten guards with Booker. The submarine, the SEAL's Zodiac boats. Wierd, it's all wierd. Booker has himself handcuffed to Maggie. She looks funny, Michael, fired up or on something. She keeps pulling away, but Booker just smacks her down and pulls her back. He's notified the press that he wants to pull his boat away from shore and race away. The whole godamned world is watching. Some NBC guy lost his head, literally. Big stink about Cassidy allowing press on this. Nobody seems to know anything about us, and the President wants to keep it that way, so we're being officially identified as part of Delta's antiterrorist force from someplace in Europe. The press bought it. Nobody's heard from Con, but I have a theory."

"Yeah. What's that?"

"He's close, very close. Booker's threatened to kill Maggie, himself, and his men if he's attacked. Basically, he wants to leave, and basically, the answer so far is definitely no."

As the sun rose higher and the day grew hotter, not much was happening to resolve the crisis. The principal players remained on the set, as it were, while just out of sight from the narrow beach, Michael and Penelope had revived considerably. All abnormal blood flows had been stopped, food and medications taken, and clean uniforms replaced the combat-torn and the blood-stained. Penelope wore a fresh jumpsuit, but she'd cut off the sleeves for comfort and more freedom of movement. Steven had joined the chopper, which now sat on the ridge road above the beach, its occupants having nothing to do at the moment.

Things began to change at 1204, when two bad guys standing on a small raft next to Booker's cigarette boat pitched forward into the water. When they floated to the surface, Booker and his henchmen saw that each of them had been shot squarely and silently between the eyes. After this brief flurry of activity near the boat, Penelope and Michael rushed to the edge of the beach, such as it was on the cliff side, where they found themselves standing less than forty feet from Maggie and Peter Coy Booker. They also arrived just in time to see two more bodyguards go down, shot from somewhere in the jungle behind them, obviously by the missing, until now, Con Duggan.

Con settled back after the second successful sniping and called directly to Michael. "Tell Booker to let her go. Tell him I'll keep shooting until he's the only one left. Then I'll come and get her myself."

"But that's what he wants you to do."

"I know, so I'm going to do it. You and Penelope be ready. Try not to get in a firefight. I've had the scope on Maggie for a long time. Her face is losing its composure. She's about to take action. Find a way to talk to her. Send Penelope if you can. If Maggie jumps the wrong way, Booker will kill her. I don't think he wants to, but he will."

Without being told, Penelope ran onto the beach and splashed into the water. Once she was thigh-deep, she dived into the gentle surf and swam steadily until she reached the hull of the cigarette boat. She grappled along the side and finally found the ladder, then pulled herself out of the water and onto the boat's deck. Dripping sea water, she brushed past the remaining guards and made her way to Booker and Maggie.

"Hello, Mags," Penelope chirped. "How's tricks?"

Maggie looked first at the bandaged shoulder, then into Penelope's eyes. They reassured and comforted her in their steady gaze. "Scary, Penelope." Her face looked taut and worried, but unafraid.

"Isn't it just, though." Penelope turned to face Maggie's captor. "Ya know, Mr. Booker, I blew up your boat once. Why aren't you dead?"

"Did you now? And how did you do that, dearie?" He looked as deranged as Caligula.

"Well, I actually just drove the bus. Steven Yank blew your boat up. Like I said, why aren't you dead?"

The question was unanswerable, but Booker replied anyway. "Perhaps in some ways, I am."

"You really ought to let her go, don't you think? I mean, there's hardly a bloody soul left alive on this freakin' island anyway. I'm shot, my Steven Yank is hurt, and Michael now only has nine little piggies left to him."

"And Con Duggan?"

The crewman closest to Penelope had the back of his head exploded that moment, and this time Penelope was spared the mess of dead flesh, but it caught Booker full in the chest.

"Con's not hurt at all, as far as we can tell." She grinned then, a slow, nasty, whorehouse grin. It was at this point that Booker felt things slip from his control. He pulled Maggie to him and withdrew a grenade from a box, pulled the pin, and held the grenade in the air with a firm grip on the handle.

"Now, if I let go of this thing, she blows up. Tell Con I want him. He can kill everybody I have left, but it's me he wants. Tell him to get down here in thirty minutes. Who knows, I might have a heart attack. That would scramble Miss Stewart every which way."

"I'll pass on your message to Mr. Duggan. But remember this, Mr. Booker: If I get a chance, I'll tear that phony hand of yours off and shove it up your ass." With as much dignity as that remark allowed, Penelope walked to the rail and dived into the water. There was another shot and another dead guard. That was evidence enough to convince the remaining guards to jump ship in the Zodiac boat, eager to surrender. Now, only Maggie Stewart, Peter Coy Booker and a hand grenade remained aboard the cigarette boat. To Booker, this was the perfect ending. Con would have to come down now. And who cared what happened after that?

With the sure knowledge that simply shooting Booker would also result in Maggie's death, Michael made his way to the boat. Now with the sun directly overhead, he stood within yards of Booker and Maggie. He wanted to make one last desperate attempt to deal with Booker and end the certainty of further casualties.

"I like your new face," Michael told Booker.

"It's a little prissy looking, I think. Don't you agree? Skin like a girl's."

"What would you say to just releasing your hostage and driving off in your little boat?"

"I'd say I wouldn't get far. That fancy chopper up on the ridge would blow me out of the water."

"Not if I tell it not to. We tried to blow you out of the water in Folkestone Harbor. It didn't work, and now a year later you're back on a boat again. But this offer isn't mine. It's from the general, the Army, and the SEAL commander, at the request of the senator. He guarantees your safety."

Booker turned to Maggie, who seemed to diminish as it grew hotter, her spirit visibly oozing out of her.

"Don't you think that's admirable, my dear? Pathetic, but admirable. The senator might have earned the right to negotiate some kind of deal, but since he basically allowed me to rape his daughter while he dallied elsewhere, not much of what he says carries a lot of weight with me.

"As for the general, what a joke and a travesty he is! He lost all his airdropped people. If Con Duggan hadn't been here, we might have even bagged ourselves a submarine. Those two men have forfeited their negotiating turf, not to mention whatever shred of personal pride they might have possessed. Besides, Con Duggan knows it has to end here, or I'll be back yet again. I came here to face him, I *want* to face him. He's my demon, you see. His companion serves the purpose of bringing the lion from the jungle. No, we'll do this my way."

"And what is that?"

"I suppose you might call it a duel. Yes, that's what it will be, a duel."

Con Duggan appeared on the narrowest part of the cliff beach. No one saw him come out of the jungle, he was just there, as if he were a trick conjured up by a wizard. His usually placid gray eyes were hard and cold, without depth, slate mirrors too complex to penetrate. For a long time, he stood there on his tiny part of the beach, and then he began to walk toward the water as the rest of the team, the newly arrived senator, and the general watched, spellbound. This is what all else had led to. Booker had wanted only one thing, and he had brought it to fruition.

Maggie jumped to her feet, pulling at the handcuff that tethered her to Booker. Booker took the cuff off his wrist, then cuffed both her wrists to the boat's steering wheel, an automobile-type wheel with a fancy leather covering. He stepped away from her, but not far, and he was still holding the grenade by its detonating handle. If he dropped it, it would blow up the boat almost at once.

"Hello, Booker. You look just like you did on New Year's Eve. You left early, and you took my date. I've come to get her back."

"And to kill me?"

"Yes, that too."

"Ahh . . . just so, and here I am. I'm going to give you the opportunity to try. If you succeed, she lives. If not, I'll blow her up with a flick of my hand. The grenade has a three-second fuse. It's harmless as long as I'm holding it. Boom, if I'm not. My proposal is simple. Many times in the past, you and I have met in shooting competitions, at most of which you placed higher than I did, but not always. It's always been a test of gun and talent against a clock. Do you recall?"

"I do, vividly. I hold a thin edge, I believe."

"Con, don't do anything he asks! Just kill him for me. Don't play games. He loves them so." Maggie's voice pierced Booker's monologue, dripping with hate, a voice so harsh Con hardly recognized it. "You know that, don't you, Con?" Her eyes were very sad.

"Yes, Mags, I know."

"Of course he does! I sent him pictures of you sprawled on your back like an open clamshell."

She pulled at the cuffs for a moment, her eyes blazing with hatred.

"Mags, I'm here. Don't worry any longer." Con's heart ached for her, and he wanted desperately to stem the hysteria that was creeping over her.

"What took you so long?" She vented her fury on him, and finally ran out of repressed emotions and sat down abruptly in the cigarette boat's seat, looking at Con. "It doesn't matter, Con. Do whatever you need to do. He raped me, but he didn't get anything for his effort. All this blood, all this shame and crap and macho killing for revenge. I'll never understand these past few days. . . . Do what you want." She leaned her head forward, resting it against her handcuffed wrists. She had opted out of the finale, but Booker meant her to be part of it.

"May I continue, now that the rudeness of my guest has run its course?" Booker said. To anyone witnessing this tableau, it would have been abundantly clear that Peter Coy Booker was totally, irrevocably over the edge. Con tried to remain calm while his stomach muscles twisted themselves into knots. What else could he do but play this, whatever *this* was, to the finish?

• • •

Booker extended a hand, the artificial one, and the ugly green hand grenade with the red tip seemed to grow. Penelope whispered to Michael as she brought her shotgun up, but he reached out his hand and pushed it down. They were standing just behind and a bit to the left of Con Duggan on the deck of the cigarette boat. All three of them faced Peter Coy Booker.

"No chance, girl." Michael patted her shoulder in sympathy.

"Very wise, Michael, very wise. . . . Here's what I propose: Con and I will have a challenge handgun contest, but with one or two differences from a normal competition. Speed is critical, of course, but this time we won't use a clock to measure it—it'll be obvious by death who wins. Secondly, there is another little twist to this contest. If Con Duggan outdraws me and shoots me, I will obviously drop the hand grenade. If, however, I outdraw Con Duggan and shoot him, I shall toss the hand grenade harmlessly into the water, far from the lovely heroine of our quest, Margaret Stuart, of the Boston Stuarts. If he beats me, resulting in my death, he has also killed the one he came to rescue. If I shoot him, he's dead, I'm alive, and so is she. In addition, you'll receive my peaceful surrender to the inept general and acquire in the process a walking, talking encyclopedia willing to provide information you couldn't possibly obtain anywhere else. I get a safe, semiluxurious—no, a safe, *very luxurious* jail somewhere.

"Really, it's simple. He kills me, she dies as well. I kill him, all manner of good things flow from my heavily laden cornucopia of criminal insight. Think of the *names* I know, the *places*, the *drugs!* To say nothing of the bad politicians all over the world. So, that's the deal. Con Duggan and I face off. You have a clear view of the possible results. Or as a twist to make it even more exciting, we face off, and the signal to shoot is the hand grenade. I throw it toward Miss Stewart, and Con finds a way to stop it in exchange for me shooting at him while he tries. Three seconds, not much time, particularly since I will have one shot. That way, there's still some possibility it will end well for the forces of good.

"Of course, Con will definitely be dead and probably Maggie Stuart as well. I've tried to be fair, don't you think? So, which will it be? I'm going to enjoy a cold drink, and when I'm finished, we compete. Fair's fair, as I see it. Choose your poison, Con Duggan."

Booker popped a can of Australian beer, a 20-ouncer. On his hip was a competition shooting rig and a custom-built .45 that had been the winning gun at the past two World Championships, the Bianci Cup, and the Steel Challenge.

Con Duggan was carrying his favorite Browning .9mm in an "Askens Avenger" holster, the kind he used on the street for concealment, not competition.

Penelope could no longer contain the rage that seethed within her. "Bloody hell, you slimy cobby from another world! That's just murder! Why not just shoot him now and surrender? Fuck all this bloody Aussie throwback! Fight *me!* That would be more of a contest than what you propose. I say we just blow you down and worry about the hand grenade later!"

"Penelope, shut the fuck up!" yelled Steven, who had finally arrived at the cliff bottom in spite of his multiple injuries.

"No, Steven Yank, I won't shut up! You get over here, and we'll take this fruitcake off his little . . ." Peter Coy Booker drew his .45, and with a perfectly placed round shattered the stock of her shotgun, knocking her flat from the impact.

"The rules are set. Take your pick. It doesn't take long for me to drink a can o' Aussie beer." Booker was clearly in the command mode at this point.

He had moved, fired, and reholstered his weapon with blinding speed, faster than Con had ever seen him shoot.

"Part of your therapy, was it Petey?" Con didn't try to conceal the contempt he felt for the man.

"Yes, it was, but don't call me Petey, Mr. Duggan. You *know* I can't abide that name."

"Mama called you Petey, isn't that right?"

"Leave my mother out of this."

"Why? It's a nice name, and it fits a game player like you."

Booker moved forward, edging a little onto the slight downslope of the cigarette boat's large deck. "Shut up or the next bullet will hit the English bitch."

"That's not part of the game, Petey. Stick to the rules—follow them real close. Mama taught you that, didn't she?"

"You know she didn't, Duggan. End this prattle about my mother!"

"Sure, Petey. I'll just check my holster, although after watching you, I don't think I can win."

"You *know* you can't win." The smirk on Booker's face was echoed in his voice.

Penelope struggled to her feet, her precious shotgun shattered, what was left of the butt resting across her bare foot.

"Jesus," she breathed, "he could easily have killed me."

Steven, more bandage than uniform, looked at her without sympathy. "That sticks-and-stones act sucks, baby. Never yell at an armed man. Shoot, then yell."

"This is crazy. This entire situation is out of a fantasy movie. I hope I'll wake up soon."

"Did you see him? The grenade never moved. He can draw and shoot just fine without a support hand." Steven was genuinely impressed by this feat.

Con motioned them to be quiet and continued, "Hey, Petey, finish your beer. I'm tired of chasing you until you catch me. Let's get it over with." Con turned his back to Booker and made an elaborate show of moving away from him. As he did so, he spoke to the 21A–C–130, 177 miles away.

"Michelle?" he whispered.

"Yes, Con."

"Is he set?"

"Scared, but set. He's never done it before. He keeps reminding me he's a pilot, not a gunfighter."

"Wish him my best. When I say go, you have .0005 seconds to pass the message and complete the action. If it works, fine. It not, we did our best. And—Michelle?"

"Yes, sir."

"Stay calm."

"Yes, sir. Calm."

"Atta girl. Put the booze on ice."

"Yes, sir. Right away."

"Not *now,* Michelle. *After.*"

"Oh, of course, sir. After."

"Remember, on *go.*"

"Yes, sir."

He had only one more command to issue. With elaborate theatricality, Con Duggan turned back to face Booker. It was like being in the rough on a televised golf shot, but there were no marshalls to clear the crowd out of the shooter's line of sight. So Con just yelled at them.

"Make way. Somebody will get hurt."

"Can't you shoot straight, Duggan?" asked Booker. Standing straight, dressed in his whites, Booker looked more like a weekend sailor than anything else, and certainly not like a gunfighter holding a small bomb in his free hand.

"Fuck it, then. Live dangerously, people." Booker waved the grenade at them.

Maggie watched from Booker's left, a few feet away. She knew Con wouldn't outdraw the man. He could, but he wouldn't. He'd sacrifice his life, and the hand grenade she'd have nightmares about for the rest of her life would be tossed overboard, and Booker would live out his life as an informant. She fixed her eyes on the crowded beach, on her father's face, grim but sure now that she at least would survive. Then she shifted her gaze to Penelope, so tough, so loyal, Maggie's baby girl. She looked at Steven and Michael, yin and yang, young and old, both of them bloodied this time, this last time, because her beloved Con couldn't survive a gunfight he was forced to forfeit for her life.

Con was wearing his oldest Marine cap, so faded and misshapen by washings and old age it was almost unrecognizable. It bore the chevrons of a Master Sargeant. He pulled it low on his face, and she couldn't see his eyes.

Loosing her composure for a moment, she screamed out his name, but he simply raised his hand and waved her to silence. He seemed to be smiling! Maggie rubbed her teary eyes on her shackled wrist and cleared them of grief momentarily. He *was* smiling.

"Remember, Duggan. If you win, she loses." Booker cast a look that was more like a leer at Maggie.

"I remember, Petey." Con stood very still, his hand far from his gun. And why not? He wasn't supposed to win. On the hill behind him, high on the ridge, something caught the sun's rays and flashed, a mirror or a windshield or . . .

"*Go!*" Duggan spat the word into his neck mike, and his cross hand went to the gun at his hip, a move so swift and silent that in the years to come some would claim he never shot at all.

Distracted, but only briefly, Booker found himself going through the mechanics of the fast draw, but even before he cleared his holster, he thought he could see the bright flash of Con's 9mm. The "go" command was translated in the precise .0005 of a second he'd asked of Michelle, and Ivan Tescher pressed the "fire" button on Steven Dye's SIKIM-1000 for the first time in his life.

Con's bullet thudded into Booker's chest, smashing his heart, while Booker's .45 fired into the deck, not even fully cleared from the speed holster. As the three-second hand grenade began to roll out of his leather hand, an EDR round, so named because of its ability to deplete energy at its source, hit Peter Coy Booker with precisely the same result Con had observed during desert training back at Nellis. For the most part, the target simply ceased to exist.

That was the case with Peter Coy Booker. One minute a large number of people had been rivetted to his face, watching for the draw. Then Ivan Tescher and the SIKIM made Booker and his hand grenade disappear without a trace. There was film of it, but no one would have believed it anyway. . . . Con had outdrawn Peter Coy Booker for the final time. Trust in a comrade's ability to rise to the occasion had overcome the odds in Booker's favor. Peace, of a sort, had come to Predator Bay on the wings of the *Whisper* and thanks to the SIKIM-1000 shooting system and the energy depletion round. So the report was worded. Yet the cost to the Confirmed Kill Team had been very high.

15

Michael Barns mopped his forehead with a bright red hand-kerchief he'd picked up at a shop in Anchorage. Sweat dripped down his neck onto his chest and back. He sat on Con and Maggie's patio, a vast concrete and stone area that Con said got so big by mistake. Con had just kept going until all the stone and concrete had been used.

"You know, Mags, I never realized until this week how hot it can get in Alaska." Michael sipped at his beer and watched Maggie move across the sightlines of his half-opened eyes to stand on the sloped lawn, her hands on her hips. She was finally filling out again after Predator Bay and looked more like the "old" Maggie every day, tanned and voluptuous yet sleek and fit as a healthy seal.

"Yes, Michael. You said that on Monday, and on Tuesday as well. Same answer: Now you know how hot it gets." The thermometer stood at an even ninety degrees at 3:00 P.M.

Then she looked out on the lake where Con was giving Ivan Tescher a lesson in water skiing. "He's not actually going to try to drag Ivan behind that boat on water skis, is he? Con knows Tesh has never been up on skis before."

"Male bonding, Maggie. Ivan Tescher shot a bad guy, so now he gets to come to your home and bond with your old man."

151

"Right, I know that. Barbarians, all of you." But she was smiling when she said it. He studied her, scanning her sexy body encased in very tight shorts and an expensive white silk blouse. She had three tiny diamonds in each earlobe and, to please Con, was wearing a diamond ankle bracelet with her sandals. Very tan against the sheer white silk and diamonds at ear and ankle, Maggie looked suited to her station in life. Queen of the roost, Con Duggan's most influential confidant, and therefore a step above them all. There were no scars, at least not visible ones. Booker had wanted her marked in ways only she would see when she looked in the mirror. She moved across the grass, shading her eyes with her hand, looking at the small stretch of rocky beach below the house.

"Look at those two! Lord, I never!" She stamped her foot, and the ankle bracelet danced with its diamonds in the sun.

"Sure you did, Mags." Michael found her reactions increasingly amusing.

"Not like that! Why, he has that poor child's bikini half off. I'm going to talk to Steven! He never leaves that child alone."

"Child? C'mon, Mags, Penelope's a lot of things, but she's long past childhood."

For a moment, a conflicted look of love, affection, and consternation crossed Maggie's face as she watched the members of the Confirmed Kill Team re-establish a sense of each other after eight months of rebuilding their physical and emotional health.

"You're right, of course. She's certainly not a child, is she? I remember the first time I met her back at Nellis. The 'party' after the first mission. Do you remember, Michael?"

"Yup. Seems like a long time ago."

"It is, in a way. When I first saw her and saw how beautiful and hungry-eyed she was, I thought of her as a rival for Con."

"What?"

"Really, Michael, *look* at her, for heavens sake. She's clearly the most desirable woman I've ever seen. Now she makes me teach her to cook and bake, talks about babies sometimes, and often calls me 'mom' instead of 'Maggie.' And Con Duggan indulges her like she was his only child."

"Not exactly. One of two—don't forget Steven."

"Oh, Steven Dye. Well, that's different. He's the boy-child, the son Con never had. Him we pass all the good stuff on to: murder, mayhem, that sort of thing."

"I'd like to remind you right here, Maggie, that *your* 'child,' Penelope James, is quite adapted to murder and mayhem herself. She seems to have been born to it."

"Yes, I suppose you're right again. She had hard beginnings she rarely talks about, but I know some of it."

"Like?"

"Michael Barns!"

"Okay, sorry. Girl stuff, I know. No men allowed. And speaking of girl stuff, how are you—really?"

"Really? Let me see. How am I, *really*?" Maggie looked out toward the lake as Con started Booker's speedboat and began to accelerate across the crystal-blue water. They had "acquired" the boat after the Predator Bay mission. It was probably the only lakebound ocean racing boat in the world. But Chapple Lake was six miles long, and the boat had plenty of room to flex its muscles. Fortunately, the EDR had vaporized Booker without scratching the boat, now renamed *Zoom Zoom* by Penelope James.

For a moment, Ivan Tescher was upright, moving smoothly along behind the boat, then the water skis went one way, and he went the other. Even above the roar of the boat's engine, Con's laughter could be heard clearly across the lake.

"I told you, Michael. Ivan Tescher should stick to helicopters."

"Probably. You were about to tell me how you are, Mags."

"Was I? Well then, physically, I'm fine. Lost some weight, as you know. At my age, I can stand it."

"You look terrific. For a while, you were thin, too thin."

"To be absolutely truthful, Michael—and I haven't even told Con this—after the Predator Bay mission ended, considering the way it ended, I didn't much care what happened to me. Oh, Con was all very supportive, as you'd know and expect him to be. He tried to hide his anger about Booker raping me by making very little of it. Truth told, the rape was expected. I expected it, at least. So I sort of detached myself from it while it happened. But how do I detach myself from all the bloodshed? It's one thing to greet Con when he comes home from a hard day of butchery in the field of international mayhem. It's quite another thing to be at the *center* of that mayhem, the target if you will, the *object* of the whole operation. That's what took the time. All those bodies, the mistakes everyone made. God, Cassidy took appalling losses."

"True, but he's been cashiered, out of the service now."

"Sure, Michael, out of the service. He's working for some tinhorn dictator in the Middle East, I hear."

"Rumors, Mags. Just rumors."

"Don't you 'rumor' me, Michael Barns. One day *he'll* be a mission."

"Hell, Maggie, I never said it wasn't a shitty, unfair world. It is, but *we're* not the shitty part. *Somebody* has to deal with the bad guys."

"Why don't you just say it, Michael?"

"What's that, Mags?"

"Why don't you just ask me if I'm going to pressure Con to get off the team?"

"Okay, are you?"

"No."

"Good."

"Don't you want to know why I'm not going to urge him to stop?"

"Not required, Maggie. I'm just relieved. Frankly, there wouldn't be a team without his leadership. The kids listen to me, but they worship and follow Con Duggan."

"I want him to stay with it because as long as men like my father are in power all over the world, the Confirmed Kill Team is always going to be a necessity."

"You dad's a U.S. Senator, Mags."

"Exactly my point." At that moment, a look of near despair and disillusionment passed briefly across Maggie's face. It was short-lived.

"Go and get them up here so we can eat. Con's the steak man, Penelope gets the ketchup, and Steven and Tesh are needed to stand around and look helplessly out of place."

"I love you, Maggie."

"I know that, Michael. I love you too. Now go get the team of the century, or I'll eat alone."

"Not here, I mean, Steven, for God's sake, Maggie's *watching* me, and you . . . oh. Now, oh . . . God, oh dear, just keep that finger dancing, oh yes . . . oh . . ."

"Am I interrupting? Maggie says come eat." Michael stepped across the panting lovers.

"Finger interruptus, or something like that," Penelope yelled after his beachward-bound back. "That's bloody awful of you, Michael! You need to get laid more!"

Michael doubled over with laughter, nearly choking on his cigarette.

Penelope seemed to be back to her old, outrageous, don't-give-a-damn self. Truth was, she'd never been far away from that self.

"Later, Steven, you'll have to finish me properly."

Still not fully recovered from his near-fatal confrontation with Chin, Steven Dye had returned from his third mission clearly the most changed of the team. He had matured immensely and seemed older, much older, than his years. Only the night before, Penelope had discovered a gray hair on him, but he claimed pubic hair didn't count. She was threatening to "look it up" somewhere.

Con Duggan had a simple theory about outdoor barbecue cooking. Your guests had their choice of how the meat was cooked: well done, medium, or rare. A polite host asked what his guests wanted, then tried to meet the request. Usually, he was successful, and complaints brought a scowl and a promise to make the miscreant cook next time.

As hungry wasps bedeviled him, Con would duck into the barbecue smoke to escape. Finally, all was in readiness, and the team was seated at the big picnic table Con had built himself. They were hungry and talkative. For the first time since Predator Bay, they could talk "shop" again.

"So, Ivan, did you enjoy using the SIKIM?" Steven Dye asked in the tone of a jealous man searching for a possible rival.

"No, I didn't," said Ivan, speaking around a mouthful of steak so rare it was nearly raw. "It scared me. I was terrified I might miss and Con would die and the boat would blow and Maggie would get hurt by the grenade."

"Delicately put, Ivan," said Maggie, her eyes twinkling with amusement.

"Thank you, ma'am." He called her ma'am most of the time. Then he returned to his favorite subject. "You can keep it, Steven. The chopper's my baby. Lots of freedom, and the world doesn't come to an end if I miss. That's the beauty of mini-machine-gun fire—lots of on-target metal."

Penelope got up and pulled up what little of her skirt there was almost to her waist. She was wearing G-string panties. "I've got a new tattoo!" she announced with glee.

"Yeah, she claims she's going to get one after every mission." Steven looked distressed. "I don't know why you have to show it, Penelope. Christ, you're practically naked."

"Oh, poo. Most everybody here has seen me bum at one time or another. We're family, ain't we?"

"Yes, Penelope, we're family," said Maggie in her "mother" voice. "But you're a very *big* girl."

Everyone laughed, but everyone looked.

"What is it? It's not very big." Con bent forward, his eyes intent on Penelope's tattoo.

"Oh, Con, it *can't* be very big. What if we go on a hundred missions? Where would I fit them all? It's a purple heart with a knife through it. I *was* wounded, you know. Bloody shot I was! So I awarded myself a purple heart."

The tattoo was on her inner thigh, very high on the leg.

"That's fine, child, now pull down your skirt." Maggie was firm but loving.

Penelope looked disappointed but did as Maggie told her. "You know," she said, "I killed twenty-nine men on that island. For the first few weeks after I got out of the hospital and was just resting at Nellis sick bay, I saw them every night in my dreams. Then the dreams got shorter, and I didn't have them so often. Finally, they stopped. Has that ever happened to you, Con?"

"Still does, honey. Just deal with it the best you can."

"I need a tattoo," said Michael, "of a foot with only four toes."

"What did you do with the toe I saved for you?"

"Penelope, I lost it that same day."

"Oh . . . I'm sorry, Michael. I was so looking forward to it as a necklace."

The Confirmed Kill Team looked at one another and simultaneously burst into laughter. Here at Chapple Lake in the pristine Alaskan sun, the return of Peter Coy Booker finally ended, and the Confirmed Kill Team was whole again. Mission three, at the deadliest cost yet, was over. Unknown to the partying guests at Con's summer picnic, mission four's roots were already taking hold.

EPILOGUE

The old "woody" station wagon, restored to its sixties glory days with painstaking care, sat to one side of a narrow canyon road. A few feet ahead of it was a Volkswagon minibus of approximately the same vintage that was apparently disabled. A man and a young woman worked at its open engine compartment. It was 4:00 in the afternoon, and the temperature had climbed to 102 degrees. The woman wore only a loose halter top and a bikini bottom. She had hair that reached to her waist, and she combed it straight and parted it in the middle in the style of the long-gone flower children. White sandals with sexy Greek straps that climbed her calves gave her a deliberately sluttish look. She was smoking a joint and drinking a quart of Bud straight from the bottle.

"They're late." The man continued to tinker at the engine compartment, though it was clear there was nothing wrong with it.

"Patience," she said, her voice husky and low, a raucous, sexy voice from an angel's face.

She turned to stare down the road, the heat simmering in rolling visible waves across the highway. She was standing at the only curve in over a twenty-mile stretch. After a five-minute wait, she saw what she was waiting for.

"Okay, here it comes," she said, an edge of nervousness creeping into her voice.

159

"Do your stuff, Jackie."

"I know what to do. I planned it, remember?"

Jackie Fox walked out into the middle of the road and staggered toward the Army two-and-a-half-ton truck that was rumbling toward them. It didn't take the driver long to realize a nearly naked woman with a beer in her hand was walking down the road, away from what appeared to be a disabled van. He brought the truck to a swerving halt.

"Hi! You guys know how to make a won't-go van into a go-go van?" she asked.

Jackie stood outside the truck driver's door, her foot high on the jump step, her ample breasts spilling out of the halter top. The view from the truck cab had its desired effect.

"What's the trouble, miss?"

"A boyfriend that's stupid, that's the trouble."

"Boyfriend?"

"Well, he picked me to stop for. He's drivin' that woody up ahead. So now I'm his girlfriend, that was the deal. He'd fix my van, I'd fuck him."

The two men looked at each other and grinned. Hot damn! Miles from nowhere and a damsel in distress! Her nipples seemed ready to pop out of the halter, and she took a long pull on the Budweiser as she eyed the two soldiers. Something wasn't right here: The two men weren't MPs, and there was no trail jeep. Just two guys driving a truck.

"Where you sports heading?"

"Toole."

"Toole?"

"Yeah, military depot."

"Ain't that the one with the gas an' stuff?"

"So they say. We're carrying truck parts and flywheels."

"Well, could you look at my van?"

"Hell yes, honey! But we can't stay. Got a sergeant that goes ballistic if we're late."

The soldiers hopped down from the truck and followed the rolling hips in the tiny swimsuit. Halfway to the van, two men stepped out from inside it carrying automatic weapons.

"Hey, what is this?" The soldiers had stopped walking and stood, perplexed, dead center on the blacktop road.

The young woman turned back toward them and waved her hand. The guns opened up without further signal and chopped the two soldiers down.

"Hurry!" Jackie Fox pulled on a pair of shorts and started to join the four additional men who had come up to the highway from below the roadbed.

"Godammit!" one of the men swore as he checked out the truck.

"What is it?"

"Your information was wrong, or your informant stiffed you."

She hurried to the truck and looked into the back. What she saw dumbfounded her: truck parts, compressors, flywheels.

"This can't be!"

"Well, it is."

"I'll kill the bastard!"

"Sure, Jackie, you kill him, but what now?"

"Now? Now we move on. Okay, we blew it. *Next* time we hit the *right* truck."

In minutes, only the empty truck and the two dead soldiers remained at the scene. They took the cargo in the hope that no one would guess what their real objective had been. Jackie Fox then went off to kill the informant who'd promised her that an altogether different load would be on that truck.

The military investigators had done their work, and the National Security people had arrived by air, the helicopter responding to the first call from the scene.

"Why did they kill them?"

"My guess is they were after something that wasn't on this truck."

"Like what?"

"Like M-55 nerve gas maybe. But I suspect we'd best get busy, because they'll be back again, whoever they are."

"Who should handle this?"

"Beats me, but it'll go straight to the President. He must have somebody, somewhere, crazy enough to get involved in stopping a gang that wants to hijack something like that."

"Nobody's that crazy!"

The senior officer glanced down once again at where the two bodies had lain, now just chalk outlines on the blacktop. "Hell, son, there's *always* somebody that crazy."

SPECIAL PREVIEW!
Introducing a masterful new epic of military adventure—the story of two families bound by one code of honor and courage . . .

AIRBORNE

"Exciting and authentic . . . puts you into the heart of battle."
                    —Marc Iverson, author of *Persian Horse*

Here is a special excerpt from this powerful new saga—available from Berkley Books . . .

Cadet Coy Vestal leaned against the wall and stared out the window of his room. From the fourth floor, he had a clear view of the Hudson River, dark and swift from the spring rains, as it surged past its verdant banks. Unusually warm weather had forced the trees to bud and bloom ahead of time, producing a profusion of color on the normally drab landscape.

Vestal watched as the graduating cadets' relatives mixed with alumni and visiting dignitaries on their way to the reviewing stands.

He had less than an hour before he would join the formation and graduate from West Point, less than an hour before he would to be a brand new second lieutenant, the first in his military family to graduate from the Academy, the first to be a commissioned officer.

His roommate was already out there with the other graduates. They were all looking forward to what would be one of the happiest days of their lives, a moment of achievement, the great beginning for which they had labored. Vestal stared out the window, waiting for some feeling of euphoria to sweep over him.

He didn't feel the joy, the excitement, the sense of achievement. He was feeling his stomach tighten from the slow constriction of his own internal pressures.

Turning from the window, he glanced across the room at the packed boxes and footlockers awaiting shipment.

Everything he owned was in these boxes, neatly packed. All his uniforms, boots, books—everything he looked to for answers was contained in the crates. He realized, as he looked over it all, how very little there was. Like the packed belongings, he was now an alien in the stark little room. He could no longer find refuge here; like these boxes, he was awaiting transport to a new location.

No doubt the uniforms, all expensively tailored and made of the finest materials, would be perfect for their call to duty, but, Vestal thought as his stomach knotted, was he?

Would the uniforms, so perfect in every detail, cover up the man inside, the man who desperately wished he wasn't leaving West Point, the man who would now be called on to perform?

He absentmindedly straightened his tunic, running his fingers over the woolen fabric. These were the last moments of privacy for the day; shortly he would become one more in a "long gray line," one more piece of the great tradition of the United States Military Academy.

As he nervously clenched and unclenched his fist, he studied the class ring on his finger. It seemed heavy, a colossal weight, as if it contained all the responsibilities and duties expected of him.

He wished his father were there. He needed a chance to talk to him, to ask him if he had ever been afraid, if he had ever felt unsure, if he had ever felt confusion. But those were questions that could never be answered. His father was long gone, a hero, fallen on the field of honor in Southeast Asia. His death and posthumous Medal of Honor had been Vestal's ticket to West Point.

Perhaps his uncles, all Airborne, all retired now as sergeants major, could answer those questions, but Vestal knew he wouldn't ask them. They were out there now with his mother, waiting anxiously to see him graduate.

He couldn't possibly admit fear, confusion, his unsure concept of himself to them. He was John Vestal's only child, his son, and the last fragment they had of their heroic brother. He couldn't let them know how he was feeling now. He didn't have the right to spoil their illusion

of who he was. And right now, that was all he really was—
an illusion of a strong military man, a new officer, a man
who knew where he was going, what he was made of,
and who would lead men into battle. He shook in his
shoes, looking back out the window as the door swung
open.

"Hey, Coy! Your uncles are downstairs waiting. They
want to walk over to formation with you."

Vestal, yanked abruptly from his thoughts, turned to face
Vince Caruso. His roommate was flushed with excitement
as he stood nervously in the door.

"I'm on my way down. You ready for your big 'moment
of truth'?" Vestal said, forcing a smile.

"That's affirmative! I am ready to shed this place and
get on with it." Caruso answered, looking at his watch.
"We better get a move on."

"Hey", Vestal reached over to pick up his hat, "I
wasn't talking about graduation. You're getting married
tomorrow, remember? That's the 'moment of truth,' when
your beautiful fiancée finds out how bad your breath is in
the morning!"

"Man," Caruso strutted in the doorway, smoothing his
tunic, "she's so dazzled by my manliness, she'll never
notice. I gotta go, she's waiting for me. Don't forget to
bring your mother to the rehearsal dinner tonight."

Vestal nodded and waved as his roommate charged off
down the hall. He walked into the hallway, took one last
glance into the room, then closed the door behind him. It
was time for the "illusion" to perform, time to close all
doors behind him and face whatever stood before him.

George Patton "Jeep" Laliker waited in front of the building,
feeling as conspicuous and uncomfortable as the bastard
child at a family reunion.

One thing was for sure, his Texas A&M uniform—the
traditional Eisenhower jacket, with the Sam Browne belt
over the gray-pink jodhpurs and highly polished brown
riding boots—stood out. He reached up and adjusted his
campaign hat, worn with this uniform only on auspicious

occasions, and tried to ignore the stares of the people passing by.

Glancing down at his watch for the fifth time in fifteen minutes, Jeep sighed and shifted nervously from one foot to the other.

The two stars on his shoulder designated his position in the Corps at A&M, Cadet Lieutenant Colonel, the highest rank possible, first in his graduating class. That position had earned him a Regular Army commission upon graduation, in a day when many of the graduates were being released to the reserves to serve their commitments. Jeep was proud of his position, proud of his high standing at A&M, but here at West Point, alma mater of past generations of the Laliker family, he was experiencing a recurring sense of failure.

This was where he had thought he would be. He had dreamed and planned since he was a child of standing here today, waiting to graduate from the Academy. He had done everything necessary to become accepted—the high grade average, the leadership positions in high school programs, participation in sports. West Point looked for the complete individual, well rounded and excelling in all areas. Jeep was a contender.

The sports had been his downfall. To become captain of his high school football team, he had taken one too many chances on the field, played with everything in him, and broken his leg in the last season. The break and subsequent lengthy healing period had cost him his slot as first alternate to the U.S. Military Academy. It had been a bitter disappointment, one that rose up in his mind and haunted him still.

Even though his family had played down his loss, encouraging him to take the scholarship to Texas A&M, he knew he was the only male member of his family, since the establishment of the Military Academy, to not attend. Admitting defeat was also not a family trait, and Jeep had hidden his disappointment, working hard to recover from the broken leg and pushing himself to the limit at A&M. He never discussed his missed opportunity at the Academy and overachieved to fill his personal void.

His father had graduated high in his class, gone into the infantry, earned his Airborne wings and served two tours in Vietnam with the 101st. On his second tour his APC had hit a land mine and he'd lost one arm and both legs. Even though he had retired from the military on a medical discharge, he kept close contact with his fellow graduates, never missing a graduation.

In years past, Mrs. Laliker had attended the ceremonies with her husband, helping him maneuver around the campus in his wheelchair, but this year Jeep's grandmother had been hospitalized the week before graduation, forcing his mother to stay behind. When she called and asked Jeep to attend, she hadn't realized the effect it would have on her son.

So here he stood, anguishing instead of celebrating. This was Senior Week back at College Station. There, he'd be going out to parties, accepting all the honor and respect he'd gained as Cadet Lieutenant Colonel. Instead, he was standing on the campus of the school he hadn't measured up to, waiting to watch graduate the men and women who would always have date-of-rank on him by one week, while his father visited with old friends in the building behind him.

To pass the time, he watched the passersby as they congregated in little groups around the walkway, waiting for the graduation parade to start. He glanced down at his watch again and was pleased to see it was nearing time for him to go back inside for his father. He turned and walked past three sergeants major standing in their uniforms by the door. He bounded up the stairs, swung open the door and collided with a cadet in the doorway, knocking the man off balance. The cadet's hat fell and rolled out on the step.

"Whoa!" Laliker said, stepping back to steady himself.

"Hey!" the startled Cadet yelled, watching as the man in front of him backed up. "Watch it! You're standing on my hat!"

Laliker looked down. Sure enough, he had planted one of his boots squarely on the brim of the cadet's hat. As he reached down to retrieve it, they bumped heads, knocking Laliker back a step. Before Jeep could apologize, the angry cadet yanked the hat from the ground, muttering under his breath, and took a long look at the offender.

As he nervously wiped at the scrape on the highly polished brim, he looked up Laliker.

"You clumsy bastard!" A twisted smile formed on his lips as he recognized the A&M uniform. "What are you dressed up for?" he asked. "A costume ball? Looks like you wore the wrong costume for this party, 'Second-stringer.'"

Laliker, incensed by the insult, squared his jaw and stepped forward. "Look, you arrogant asshole, I—"

"Gentlemen!" A voice barked out from behind them.

They both turned to see who was speaking. A gray-haired major, who bore a striking resemblance to the A&M cadet, scowled at them both from his wheelchair. The West Point cadet came to attention and saluted as Laliker stepped past him and stood behind the chair.

"Sir," the cadet stammered, pushing the door open, "allow me."

Major Laliker returned the salute and nodded as Jeep, eyes blazing, pushed the wheelchair past and down the ramp.

The cadet hurriedly joined some older men and rushed past the Lalikers to the formation. Jeep watched, still stinging from his slur, as he pushed his father toward the reviewing stands in silence. After the chair had been placed on the stand, Jeep walked around and stood beside his dad.

Major Laliker had been glancing through the program, giving his son time to cool down. He cleared his throat. "You want to talk about that?" he said, looking up at Jeep.

"No, I expected it!" Jeep said angrily.

The major shifted uncomfortably in the chair. "Get the chip off your shoulder, son. It doesn't become you. He didn't mean what he said."

"The hell he didn't!"

"Look," Major Laliker said, as the band struck the first chords of a march and the parade began, "he's strung tight today; so are you. Just write it off to nerves. I saw his name tag and looked him up. That's John Vestal's son. He's probably a good man."

"Vestal?" Jeep questioned, looking down at his father. "He graduated with you?"

"No, John Vestal was a master sergeant and died in Viet-Nam. He was awarded the Medal of Honor."

"Just because his dad died to get him into the Academy, doesn't mean he's a 'good man.' "

"Well, you could be right. At any rate, you'll have the opportunity to find out soon enough. You're both headed in the same direction," Major Laliker said, looking out over the cadets as they marched by. "The program has the destination of each cadet next to his name. Just like you, Coy Vestal is headed for Ranger School and the 82nd Airborne Division."